SCORPION DAWN

A HELLION HOUSE NOVELLA

EMMA JANE HOLLOWAY

INTRODUCTION

When the prey becomes the hunter …

Miranda Fletcher lives in a glittering world of aeronauts and artists, dance cards and dandies, but terror lurks outside the city walls. The countryside is infested with hungry abominations called the Unseen, and a single crack in the capital's defenses invites disaster.

Then Miranda witnesses a murder and learns the walls aren't as secure as their magical protectors claim. But despite a string of bloody crimes, no one is foolhardy enough to question the mages, much less battle monsters at the gate.

Except Miranda. When tragedy shatters her home, she'll risk everything to get answers—and vengeance. Sometimes the smallest creature carries the deadliest sting.

Hope has two beautiful daughters; their names are Anger and Courage. Anger at the way things are, and Courage to see that they do not remain as they are.
— Saint Augustine of Hippo

CHAPTER 1

"Watch for a moment," Norton Fletcher said to his son, Gideon. "Then we'll bow and scrape to the Conclave. I'd rather see this than their sour faces."

Side by side, they ran down the stairs of the administration building and took a shortcut across the airfield. Representatives from the Conclave had arrived thirty minutes ago, their presence like a house call from an anxiety dream.

Gideon's stomach ached with worry. "Will they take the delay as an insult?"

"Probably."

"Then why take the risk?"

"This is my place," Fletcher replied. "Mine. They don't have the power here."

Gideon wasn't sure that was true—not in any way that mattered. Still, he couldn't help looking over to where his father pointed one gloved hand.

Far ahead, a shout rose from the crowd of workers as mooring ropes released and the *Scorpion* floated skyward, sleek and nimble. Twin balloons hung one above the other, the silk striped midnight blue and silver above a narrow, high-prowed gondola. The feather-shaped crest of Fletcher Industries was visible along the side, even from where Gideon stood at the edge of the field.

"A beauty, isn't she?" Fletcher said, adjusting the brim of his gray top hat. Of middling height, he was stocky and weathered by decades in the wind and sun. He had begun his career as an airman, then built his highly profitable empire one dirigible at a time. "I took her up myself yesterday. Still a few improvements to make, but she'll be perfect for quick travels inside the city walls. Clever thing can fly right between buildings with a good pilot. Only needs one or two crew members to run it."

Gideon had seen the *Scorpion* under construction, but this was his first glimpse of it in flight. The ship was perfect for a rich man in a hurry or a young buck eager to show off. With the new restrictions on long-distance flight, building urban airships was a smart business move—but that was Fletcher, always one innovation ahead of his peers.

As his heir, Gideon was both eager and humbled. "What's its range?"

"Depends on the weather. It could fly to the next city, but that would be chancy."

Gideon shaded his eyes, admiring the graceful way the ship turned. The sight captured his world at its best. Scents from the surrounding fields and work sheds mixed in a familiar, throat-catching way. He'd been around airmen and their machines for the last twenty-five years—since he'd been a babe in arms.

"The name *Scorpion* was Miranda's idea," Fletcher said. "She's been showing an interest in the business lately."

"How so?" Gideon asked, never knowing what to expect from his youngest sister.

By unspoken agreement, they altered their course toward the edge of the property, where their unwelcome guests waited. No trees stood around the airfield, but the shrubs and brambles along the outskirts flamed October gold and scarlet in the slanting sun. The early afternoon was still warm despite a bite in the air that promised frost.

"She's been practicing at the shooting range." Fletcher waved a hand toward the airfield's training grounds. "And she's been flying with the junior crew."

Gideon couldn't suppress a smile. Miranda loved the air as much as he did. "I knew she was coming here, but not the details. How is she progressing?"

"I'd give her a real job if she wasn't my daughter."

"But?"

Gideon already knew the answer. Most professions had women in their ranks, but the wealthiest families still preferred to keep their daughters at home.

Fletcher cleared his throat. "Thank the gods your mother's not alive to see her youngest covered in grease and gunpowder. She'd accuse me of negligence."

There were volumes of family arguments in those words—what Miranda wanted versus what she'd be allowed to have—but Gideon left those for later. They'd arrived at the spot where a handful of Fletcher's employees toiled.

"The repairs are almost done," Gideon said. "It was a hard job."

"But the men made fast work of it," his father replied. "Remind me to stand them a round next time they visit the tavern."

One of the morning's delivery carts had rolled free as it was being unhitched. As the story went, a rabbit had spooked the big draft horses, and the idiot beasts had thundered away from the flop-eared menace at top speed. The harness—buckles half-undone in the driver's hands—had come free, but the resulting jolt had unlocked the wagon's brake. The heavy load of iron fittings had rolled free before crashing into the wall bordering the airfield's land, knocking a gap in the old stone. Humans, horses, and bunny were unhurt, though the wagon was beyond redemption.

And more than the physical wall had broken. The accident had smashed the Conclave's handiwork as well—hence the visit. A delegation from the Citadel, the Conclave's stronghold at the center of the city, stood grim-faced on the sidelines. They had insisted on personally assessing the damage to the wall the moment they'd arrived.

The sight of them blackened Gideon's mood. Two of the visitors were dressed in dark coats and bowler hats, marking them as administrative flunkies. The other three wore mage's robes—two in black and one in the pale blue of the Senior Council. A handful of liveried Conclave guards stood a polite distance away, frowning at the grubby laborers but not offering to help.

Gideon recognized the blue robe as Councilor Ormond, a heavy-jawed boulder of a man with small, wide-spaced blue eyes.

Ormond looked up as they approached. "You are certain nothing penetrated from the other side? The breach was hours ago. There's been opportunity for intrusion."

Fletcher's jaw jutted forward defiantly. Still, he kept an affable tone. "My men have been watching constantly with orders to shoot anything that moves. Nothing has set foot on our side."

A brief silence fell, broken only by the sound of stone being shifted into place. The twenty-foot wall was hundreds of years old—one of the original sections of the barrier that circumnavigated the city. Each block had been meticulously cut to fit, like an enormous puzzle.

All the same, it wasn't chiseled rock that kept the city safe. The barrier around the town was made from many materials— wood, hedges, wrought iron, and even barricades made from whatever rubble the slums could spare. None of it was secure against the enemy outside—not completely. It was the Conclave's magic that made it impregnable.

Until, of course, a reckless rabbit had turned a wagon into a battering ram.

"Your carelessness risked the entire city," Ormond said, his voice dark with warning.

"It was pure bad luck," Fletcher replied. "If there's a fine, we'll pay it."

The councilor shot him a glare of pure disdain. "Spoken like a merchant."

Fletcher colored but was interrupted before he could retort.

"We're ready, sir," called a voice from above. Three airmen stood on top of the repaired section of the wall, wearing heavy work gloves and brown coveralls. Gideon recognized the speaker as Higgins, a senior crew hand.

"Are you certain it's sound?" Fletcher shouted back.

Higgins stomped a foot on the stone. "Tight as a banker's fist, she is."

Fletcher nodded to the Conclave's men. When Ormond moved his fingers slightly, the two black-robed acolytes stepped toward the wall. One bore a satchel. From it, he took tiny pliers and snips, along with rolls of fine silver-colored wire. With deft movements, the acolytes began to mend the mesh that ran inside the barrier like an enormous, magic-conducting spiderweb.

The Conclave's protective power flowed from their Citadel into the silver mesh that circled the city. No unnatural creature could climb, fly, or burrow past the protective shield. It was all that stood between the city and the monsters outside.

With ropes and harnesses, Higgins and Crewman Yale helped the acolytes scale the wall, heaving them up a foot at a time as they made their repairs. The interaction between the two groups was cool with suspicion. No one exactly knew what Conclave did inside the Citadel. Magic, certainly, but what else?

Torture and execution, Gideon thought. Not long ago, he'd rescued a man—Joseph Ellery—from beyond the wall, but Ellery had vanished into the Citadel's dungeon, condemned because magic ran in his blood. Fortune-tellers, hedge wizards, and wise women shared similar fates. Only the Conclave was allowed to wield magic. A quiet, studious man, Ellery had perished to prove that point—and to save his gifted daughters from the same fate.

Gideon's jaw ached as he bit down on the memory, forcing himself to focus on the work above. The acolytes were near the top of the wall now, repairs nearly complete. Higgins and the others reeled them in, fearless of the height—they spent their time in the sky, after all.

One of the acolytes was a good climber. The other hung from the ropes like a sack of meal, relying on the airmen to heave him upward. As they neared the top, he began kicking and groping for handholds like a small child struggling in the bath. Apprehension tightened between Gideon's shoulder blades. Without thinking, he found a foothold between the stones and began climbing one of the ropes, heedless of his well-tailored clothes.

Before Gideon was halfway up, Crewman Black, one of the new recruits, bent to catch the acolyte's waving hand. It was a mistake.

Gideon did not see the acolyte make his flailing surge to the top, but he saw Black topple backward, arms wind-milling as he tried to catch his balance. Heart plunging, Gideon scrambled up the last few feet. *"Black."*

The crewman screamed as his feet kicked into empty air.

Gideon crouched atop the narrow stones. The drop to the other side should have been fatal, but a thick growth of broom and juniper partially broke the man's fall with a crackle of snapping branches. Black rolled off the greenery, then sprawled in the long, unkempt grass, legs twisted awkwardly beneath him. Gideon's stomach lurched. It was impossible to tell if the man's limbs were broken, or even if he were still alive.

Meanwhile, the acolyte blubbered with shock and vertigo. Higgins held the man by the shoulders, his expression grim. "What shall I do with this one?"

"Get him out of here," Gideon ordered, half-tempted to push the acolyte over the edge.

Perhaps reading his tone, Yale and the others hastened to obey.

Gideon calculated the distance between Black and the edge of the lurking forest. There was a thirty-foot stretch of grass and weeds before all visibility was lost. As long as Gideon could see around him, he might be safe.

"Find me a harness," Gideon called. "I'll put it on Black, and you can pull him up."

"No, sir," Higgins said, rubbing the gray bristle along his jaw.

"Why not?"

Black was not yet twenty—barely at the start of his life. He was worth the risk.

"There's your reason." The older man pointed. "I'd rather you asked me to find you a rifle."

Gideon followed his pointing finger. What he saw made an abyss of fear open inside him.

CHAPTER 2

The monsters had come.

There were many things living in the forest beyond the wall, and Gideon had seen a fair few from the deck of his father's airships. The Great Disaster had born strange fruit, but the Unseen were the worst. No one knew where they'd come from, or why they existed at all. Folklore spawned tales of disease and damnation, but chemists and doctors claimed nothing could be caught from their bite. Except death, of course. They were predators that wore human—or at least *humanish*—faces.

Two Unseen stood at the edge of the trees—a male and female holding hands. Their hair was white—the male's completely so, the female's streaked with a reddish brown. Still, they seemed young, though their appearance was too alien to be certain. They were tall and painfully slender, their skin bloodlessly white. Dark shadows bruised the hollows of their cheeks and beneath their colorless eyes. They wore clothes, but they were ill-fitting, as if they'd been stolen. Such thievery was possible—Crewman Yale had once said the Unseen were either crazy and brutish or clever and lethal. By the cautious glares these two gave the airmen, Gideon was willing to bet the pair was trouble.

He watched as the male flexed and curled his free hand. It was the only movement either made. It—*he*—had claws as long as finger joints. The female's gaze fixed on Black. She was strangely beautiful, but in a way that made nightmares of his dreams.

"There are only two," Gideon murmured, rising to his full height. The wall was just a foot wide and woefully uneven, but he'd spent his life in the rigging. He could all but balance on thin air.

"It's a trap," Higgins said. "There are others hiding in the trees. It took a while, but eventually the hungry beggars noticed us working on the wall. They've been waiting like hounds under the table, hoping one of us would fall like a scrap of bacon."

"Did they try to attack?"

Higgins shrugged. "We shoot before they make it past the tree line. That's kept them back, but each time they're bolder than before."

And Black, helpless and alone, was enough of a tempting meal to make the risk worthwhile. Neither man needed to say it.

The male's eyes turned Gideon's way, making him wonder if the creature had heard and understood the conversation.

"Here you go, sir," Yale said, passing a rifle to Gideon.

Gideon took it, grateful for its solid weight. He checked to ensure it was loaded and ready to fire.

"What's going on up there?" Norton Fletcher called from below.

Gideon glanced down to see identical scowls plastered across Ormond and Fletcher's faces. Irritation struck. He didn't have time for explanations. "Wildlife."

Higgins gave a shout. Gideon returned his attention to the field to see the distraction had cost him. The female had darted forward, grabbed Black's arms, and was dragging him toward the trees. Black regained consciousness and screamed in pain, but agony was soon pushed aside by visibly dawning horror. No one survived the Unseen. No one wanted to. *Hungry bastards.*

Black's struggles frustrated the female, who bent to get a better grip on her prey. Her grimace showed pointed teeth, like a pale, pretty shark. Blood scored Black's arms where her claws had dug in.

The male pushed in, taking over. With unreal strength, he hauled Black up by the waist, clutching him to his chest like an oversized toy. The female leaned in, licking Black's face.

The youth's screams turned into a heart-rending howl. She reared back, her face splitting into a mocking grin.

Gideon raised the rifle, cursing the tremor in his hands. Fletcher airships had flown plenty of missions to pluck sailors from the river when things went wrong. He'd seen what happened if the rescue ship arrived too late. There was a code, a promise every airman made to his fellows—no one let his friends be taken alive.

He shot with both barrels, blowing Black apart. The male, too. Blood and bone exploded into the air. Even through his ringing ears, Gideon thought he heard the sound of rending flesh, then the patter of it raining to the ground. That was impossible, and yet his mind supplied every vivid detail.

He crouched, a wave of dizziness swamping his senses. He'd never fired on his own men. Not before now.

He'd hardly known Black, but that didn't matter. Gideon had ripped the crewman's life away.

I killed him.

A boy.

A mercy.

A murder.

No court would convict Gideon for saving a lad from the forest. For a moment, he wished they would.

A visceral chill left him shaking, but it cleared his head. Guilt and hatred rushed through him. If it hadn't been for the acolyte… Yet, they desperately needed the barrier. There would be no retribution for the clumsy move that had sent Black to his death. The Conclave was beyond the reach of common justice.

Higgins pulled the rifle from Gideon's hand, then began reloading it. Something new was happening below. The female circled the ruined bodies of the others, as if she didn't believe what had just passed. At the same time, more of the Unseen crawled from the forest, some on two feet and others on all fours. These were not pale and beautiful, like the first pair, but were ragged and twisted, with dark, matted hair and hunger-glazed eyes. According to Yale's classification, these would be the crazy ones.

They rushed the bloody mess, spittle dripping from their jaws. The female whirled on them, slashing her claws and screeching her displeasure. Gideon blinked. *She's protecting what's left of her mate.* It was a disquieting thought, too human for comfort.

Then the female lifted her pale gaze to Gideon and howled, showing her teeth. Both clawed hands reached toward the airmen on the wall, the bloody nails as sharp as knives. Obedient to her command, the Unseen charged.

A horrid realization slammed Gideon. The wire had been repaired, but not recharged with magic. "The barrier is down," he shouted. "*Get off the wall.*"

Higgins blasted the shotgun into the swarm, but no one remained to see what he'd hit. Gideon grabbed a rope and slid down it, feeling the burn of hemp against his palms. The others followed, hitting the ground and scrambling away from the wall. The cacophony of snarling, mewling madness drifted after them. Gideon grabbed the fresh rifle Yale offered.

"Let us work." Councilor Ormond stepped forward, flanked by the black-clad acolytes.

Gideon didn't argue. Instead, he retreated farther to make room. Ormond faced the repaired section of the wall, close enough to reach out and brush it with his fingertips. The acolytes flanked him, and the guards formed a loose half-circle behind the trio, rifles drawn.

"It's about bloody time they did something besides glare," Gideon muttered to his father. He flinched as he heard the Unseen's claws scraping the stone. They were climbing. The urge to run burned white-hot inside Gideon, but he cocked the rifle. His father put a calming hand on his arm.

"Stay strong," Fletcher murmured. "The men have lost one of their own. Show them your courage. They need it."

Gideon swallowed hard, wanting to scream at Ormond to hurry. The councilor made complicated gestures in the air while all three mages chanted. Nothing in their manner spoke of urgency.

The Citadel guards trained their weapons on the top of the wall. They didn't have long to wait. The top of a scraggly head popped into view, and the rifles thundered. Another face reared above the stones, then another and another, clawed hands scrabbling for a hold. Volley after volley sounded, drowning out howls of pain and fury. The stink of gunpowder filled Gideon's nose. Dropping to one knee for a better angle, he took his own shot, grunting at the kick of the rifle against his shoulder.

Then a distant silver flare glimmered in the corner of his vision, where the wall curved far to his right. The glow sped toward the repair, rippling as the magic of the Citadel coursed along the silver mesh. The spell was taking hold. A cry went up as others saw light flowing from the left as well, the two halves straining to knit the shield together. With a sound like a giant *crack*, the lines of magic met.

Gideon ducked, the radiant flash blinding him. Behind his eyelids, an afterimage of the wire burned bright. Cries of shrill agony rang from the other side of the wall, then the Unseen fell silent.

The humans cheered.

Gideon straightened, blinking. No more faces leered over the wall. They were safe. The Conclave guards parted, and the three robed figures turned as one.

"It is done," Ormond said.

A scatter of images flashed through Gideon's mind—the nightmare beauty, Black screaming, the fury in the bereaved creature's eyes. Her mad howl had felt like a curse settling on Gideon's soul, personal and bloody. *She wants revenge.*

The fugue was broken by his father stepping forward and bowing low. Humility looked odd on Fletcher, but Gideon knew, without a doubt, his father meant it. The Conclave had just saved their lives.

A tiny, irrational piece of Gideon resented it.

"Our profound thanks to you, Councilor Ormond, for your timely assistance," Fletcher said.

Ormond gave a slight nod, which seemed to serve as a signal. The acolytes broke away to pack up their tools and supplies.

Higgins and Yale gave the order for the other Fletcher Industries workmen to begin cleaning up the detritus of the repair. Already, they were making plans to get blind drunk in Black's honor. Gideon would not join them. Not tonight—not when he could still smell the gunpowder from the fatal shot.

The Fletchers and the Conclave representatives moved away to give the workers room. As they walked, Ormond waved a hand to encompass the scene. "We have kept the city safe since the Citadel's founding, but the barrier's protection cannot be taken for granted."

Fletcher bowed again, accepting the reproof. "As you say."

"I had to shoot one of my men," Gideon said, voice harsh with grief. "None of us is likely to forget."

Fletcher shot him a sharp glare, silently telling him to hold his tongue.

Ormond cocked his head, studying Gideon. "I am sorry your crewman lost his life, but there are always consequences for such use of power. Whether we like it or not, magic demands a price."

Gideon's throat closed as if he'd been punched in the windpipe. The words had cracked open a doorway, and beyond lay a world of doubt. Had Black fallen by accident, or had his death been fuel for the spell?

Ormond held up a hand. "I can see in your eyes you suspect a sinister act. There was no such thing. That's simply how magic works—the power of it has to come from somewhere."

"Death?"

"Power takes what it needs. Each spell has its own appetite." The councilor patted Gideon's chest with the flat of his hand. "Be more careful in the future. The forest isn't the only home to hungry creatures."

Gideon sucked in a breath to demand more explanation, but his father gripped his arm with bone-crushing strength. They remained silent as the members of the Conclave took their leave, robes billowing around them like wings. A pair of carriages waited at the edge of the airfield. Fletcher did not release Gideon's arm until the driver whipped up the matching gray horses.

"Did you hear what he said about Black?" Gideon asked darkly.

Fletcher's face was drawn tight. "The boy paid a price for our safety. Don't throw that away by making an enemy of Ormond."

"It might be too late for that." Gideon frowned. *The forest isn't the only home to hungry creatures.* What the bloody hell did that mean?

"The wall is fixed, and we only lost one man." Fletcher poked Gideon in the chest, right where Ormond had patted him a minute ago. "Be grateful."

His father strode across the field toward the *Scorpion*. The ship still bobbed in the blue sky, oblivious to the chaos below. Gideon leaned on his rifle, wishing he'd been in the sky that afternoon. Anywhere but in the company of monsters and mages.

The Conclave wasn't the government, priests, or representatives of the law—yet they'd assumed the power of all three, issuing edicts and punishing those who disagreed. And who would dare to protest when magic was the only shield against the Unseen? It had been this way since the Great Disaster, hundreds of years ago.

Home to hungry creatures. The phrase repeated in Gideon's mind.

He had been forced to shoot an innocent man. Was that *truly* necessary to feed the barrier's magic? Or had Ormond said that just to twist the knife in his soul?

A mix of guilt and doubt left the taste of ashes in Gideon's mouth. He straightened, hoisting his rifle, and set out across the airfield.

Inside his skull, Black still screamed.

CHAPTER 3

"I never ask you for anything," Miranda Fletcher said a week later. She hurried to keep up with Gideon, dodging a newsboy and a penny-farthing bicycle as they crossed the street.

"I beg to differ. You asked me to pay for your tea and sandwiches barely an hour ago," Gideon replied. "As a grown woman of two-and-twenty, I would think you'd have pocket money of your own."

Miranda brushed a fleck of soot from her sky-blue coat. "I'm not talking about trifles. This is important."

Without slowing his pace, Gideon walked backward a few steps, hands in his pockets. He met her indignant glare with one eyebrow raised. "Lunch seemed critical enough as you were gobbling it down."

"Never mind lunch. I'm talking about the Mortons." Miranda met her brother's brilliant blue eyes. He was dark-haired, handsome, and the heir to an airship empire—just the perfect leverage she needed. "Kitty Morton likes you. I want to get my hands on the Mortons' telescope, and you are the key to an invitation to their home."

16

"I can't believe you have so little regard for my virtue."

"If I was inquiring into your virtue, I'd be after a microscope instead."

Gideon laughed, which was the object of Miranda's game. The infectious sound turned heads as they strode briskly down the street. Miranda caught his sleeve, drawing him closer. She knew about what had happened at the airfield—everyone did—and was all too aware of the impact on Gideon's spirits. Her brother was a champion when it came to brooding.

"I'm serious," Miranda chided. "Kitty's mother will invite us if she thinks you're a potential suitor. Dance with Kitty at Sidonie's engagement party. Dance with her twice, and we'll be in the game."

"Have you truly grown so mercenary?"

Miranda raised her gloved hands in surrender. "I want access to their observatory."

"Why the sudden interest?"

"I need to improve my navigation skills if I'm ever going to take an airship outside the city. Therefore, I need to study the stars. The Mortons have the best equipment, but Mrs. Morton dislikes me."

"That's because you are smarter than she is, and you won't hide the fact."

"I do try to spare her," she replied. "Honestly, I do."

"I don't believe you."

"I can only do so much when the woman has a mind like a dry well. There's nothing there but echoes and the occasional spider."

He shrugged. "Perhaps, but you'll have to butter up the Mortons yourself if you want to play with their toys. I'm not your Trojan horse, sister dearest."

"You're no fun."

"You're simply trying your best to annoy me."

"Did it work?"

Her brother rolled his eyes.

Miranda hid a smile. She was glad she'd convinced him to go out with her for the day. She'd had to sacrifice a dressmaker's appointment with her sister, Sidonie, but no effort was too small if it put an end to Gideon's gloom. It had put the whole household on edge.

"Where are we going again?" she asked.

"You'll see."

The October sky was mottled with pewter clouds. The temperature had been dropping since noon, and the air was thick with moisture. Miranda could almost feel the fog waiting in the alleyways like a patient cat. Night came early this time of year—and this wasn't the best part of town to be in when darkness fell. Suspiciously, she glanced at the streets around her. Buildings crowded the narrow road, their storefronts barely wide enough for a door.

"This is the bookstore I was telling you about," Gideon replied, finally coming to a halt.

Miranda gratefully stopped, the skirts of her new fawn-colored walking dress settling around her. She'd kept up with Gideon's long strides despite her bustle and high-heeled boots, but the opportunity to pause was welcome.

Dobson and Son Booksellers sat on the corner of White Street and Oak Lane. The building was two stories high, half-timbered, and caked with soot and grime. Still, it was enticing. In Miranda's view, any place with books was.

She leaned in, her breath fogging the dirty glass of the bay window. "I wonder if they have anything on astronomy?"

"Probably. This shop has books on everything."

Some of the volumes displayed in the window appeared expensive, with leather bindings stamped in gold leaf. Others had modest cloth or paper bindings that ordinary workers could afford. The best, however, seemed ancient and full of secrets. Miranda did a quick mental calculation of the space available on her bookshelves at home. There wasn't much.

A brass bell rang with a polite tinkle as Gideon opened the door and steered her through. Miranda craned her neck as she stepped inside, scanning the floor-to-ceiling shelves. To the left of the door was an ancient oak desk. Behind it perched a withered man in a green waistcoat and wire-rimmed spectacles.

"Miranda, may I introduce Mr. Dobson?" Gideon said. "Dobson, this is my sister, Miss Miranda Fletcher."

"I'm pleased to meet you," Miranda said.

Smiling, the older man bobbed his head in greeting.

"Are you the founding Dobson or his son?" she asked.

"I am the son, Miss Miranda, and I have served behind this counter since I left school."

"That is why he is such a treasure," Gideon said. "If I want something—anything—he knows how to locate a copy."

A watery sunbeam shone through the transom above the door, illuminating clouds of dancing dust motes. Miranda breathed in the scent of paper and old bindings. Books printed outside the city were expensive, since most were shipped by dirigible. Anything obscure was almost impossible to find. Dobson had a treasure trove, and she wanted to devour each and every volume.

"How much time do we have?" she asked her brother, running a finger along the closest spines.

"I brought you here to see something in particular," Gideon said, exchanging a look with Dobson.

"Oh?" Miranda noticed a stairway leading upstairs with a sign proclaiming—*Gentleman's Suite Available for Rental.* She wondered if a lady could move in, even just to sit and read.

"Come into the back," Gideon said with a smile. "I know you like history every bit as much as the stars."

Her brother must have prearranged the visit, because Dobson slipped off his stool and locked the street door without a word. Then he beckoned them through a heavy curtain that hung behind the desk. Miranda followed, mystified as the bookseller drew the blinds and lit a lamp that hung from the ceiling. A table ran the length of the narrow room, probably for sorting the books piled in tottering stacks everywhere she looked.

Dobson went to a battered cabinet set against the wall. Its drawers were wide but shallow, each marked with a handwritten label in a brass holder. He pulled one open, then carefully withdrew a large sheet of heavy paper, which he then spread on the table. Intrigued, Miranda drew closer. It was a map of the city, but an incredibly old one. Up close, she could see the paper was actually fine vellum, carefully inked and colored.

"This dates to ten years before the Great Disaster. You can see the spire of the Citadel here." Dobson pointed to a spot just north of the river. "The site has always been a place of great power. It was a cathedral back then, and a temple of the goddess Diana before that. They called the site Lan Diana. That's where the city name originates from—LanDian. The Conclave renamed it Londria when they finished the wall."

Miranda leaned yet closer, her heartbeat speeding as the old bookseller spoke. It was plain why Gideon had brought her to see the map. She adored history, and this was something extremely rare. Almost nothing so fragile had survived from before the Disaster.

The sight of the Citadel's spire on the ancient map was strange. The Conclave had taken the old building for their own, adding to some parts while repurposing what was already there for others—although no one knew exactly what was inside.

"You'll notice the streets are different on the map," Gideon said. "They run every which way."

He was right. The main streets of the modern city ran from the Citadel to the barrier like the spokes of a wheel, carrying protective magic in an unbroken web of silver. As the city expanded, the streets and walls were altered with orderly precision, while bridges were positioned along the river to ensure the lines of power stayed unbroken.

"Some streets have changed," Dobson agreed, "but it's surprising how much has not."

The bookseller angled the map toward Miranda, ensuring she had a good view. Their eyes met and, despite their differences of age and station, it was clear they shared a love for ink and old paper. She gave him a conspiratorial smile and he winked.

"I wonder." Gideon leaned over the table, his dark hair falling over his forehead. "The rivers—the small ones. Are they unchanged?"

Miranda gave him a curious stare. "Why would the course of the rivers change?"

Dobson tapped the map. "Waterways silt up and are dredged, not to mention what building and excavation can do."

"The wall runs along here," Gideon said, tracing his finger from the Fletcher airfield south of the city, over the eastern river docks, and then in a loop around the north. "Here, a minor tributary crosses the line where the barrier is now."

"So?" Miranda asked.

He tapped the vellum. "The waterway is on the map, but it's not visible now."

"The Ty was covered over after it left the heath," Dobson said. "It happened long before you were born."

"But it's there somewhere, under the earth."

Miranda guessed what her brother was thinking. Since the incident at the airfield, Gideon's mind had circled around one topic—whether the barrier was actually secure.

"Every child is taught that the Conclave's magic prevents anything evil from burrowing beneath the wall or flying above it," Miranda said. "Why would that change if a river got buried?"

"The barrier broke when the wall was smashed. What if the spell was intended to span a river, but then the river went away? Would that create a breach?"

She watched his face carefully, trying to follow his reasoning. "Wouldn't the Conclave notice?"

"What if they repaired it on the surface, but there was a deeper weakness?"

"You're seeing terrors where they don't exist, Gideon. I'm about to lose one sibling when Sidonie gets married. Please don't make me lose another to nervous collapse."

His expression said she'd entirely missed his point.

"Respectfully, sir," Dobson said. "I would be careful what you say beyond this room. There are always those willing to twist the words of anyone discussing such matters."

Heaving a sigh, Gideon stepped back. "Then I need to talk less and dig deeper."

Miranda wanted to ask precisely what he meant, but Dobson's warning had put her on edge. She would wait until she had Gideon alone.

The bookseller put the map away while Miranda returned to the main part of the store, eager to peruse the shelves. She began at the bookcase closest to the bay window, but was momentarily distracted by the street outside. A milk wagon and a cart filled with geese were at an impasse, neither giving way. Then she recognized a figure hurrying down the street. Rapping on the glass, she caught his attention and waved.

Dr. Richard Wilcox was her sister Sidonie's fiancé, and one of the most handsome men Miranda knew. He was tall and slender, his ebony skin and dark eyes striking against the dove gray of his frock coat. He was dressed to go visiting, but he carried his doctor's bag. Miranda guessed he'd been summoned to an unexpected emergency. A grubby boy trotted beside the doctor, no doubt the messenger who had summoned him.

As soon as he saw her, Dr. Wilcox turned his steps toward the shop. Dobson, emerging from the back of the store with Gideon on his heels, hurried to unlock the door.

The doctor pushed inside, nearly bowling Dobson over in his haste. Cool air swirled in behind Wilcox, bringing the scent of smoke and horses into the shop. Papers fluttered on the oak counter.

"Miss Miranda," the doctor said with a bow. "It is a pleasure to see you."

"The pleasure is ours, doctor," she replied, noting the boy had remained outside, fidgeting with impatience. "Please don't let us keep you if you have an urgent case."

"My reasons for stopping are selfish," Wilcox replied, turning to Gideon. "I'm glad to see you here."

Her brother's eyes widened with surprise. "For what reason?"

"I may need your help."

"Why?" Gideon asked, but then his confusion dissolved under the doctor's steady gaze. "Do you have one of your special cases?"

"From the information I have thus far, I'd say yes."

"What cases would those be?" Miranda asked, annoyed to find herself in the dark.

The glance Wilcox gave her was oddly nervous. He turned back to her brother, a question in his eyes.

"I am not invisible," Miranda said crossly. "What are you two up to?"

Gideon started for the door. "Stay here. I will be back in an hour or so to escort you home. I'm sure you can find something to amuse yourself." He gave a significant gesture at the towering shelves lining the room.

"Of course," Miranda said with heavy sarcasm. A flush of anger rose to her cheeks. She disliked being left behind like an unwanted parcel to be retrieved at her brother's convenience.

"Forgive me," Gideon said, kissing her forehead. "It's a medical emergency."

The two men charged out the door, following the messenger boy at a run. Miranda leaned out of the bookseller's shop, watching their retreating backs. Her brother had the medical skills of a turnip. Why on earth would he be required so urgently?

"I find," Dobson said, taking up his position behind the oak desk, "that answers rarely come when called. One typically has to go fetch them."

Miranda raised her brows. "You do not feel such curiosity would be a breach of propriety?"

Dobson peered over his spectacles. "I am a bibliophile. What do I know of propriety?"

She grinned. "Quite right."

Miranda ran after her brother.

CHAPTER 4

Annoyance gave Miranda energy, and she quickly began to catch up to the two men. Again, she wondered why Wilcox had asked for Gideon's help. Her brother knew something she did not.

Miranda had to rectify that at once.

Even so, when Dr. Wilcox and her brother made a left turn, she hesitated. Maudlin Way—where the men were going—was no place for a well-bred lady. Little more than a narrow, winding alleyway, its ramshackle buildings leaned toward one another as if engaged in conversation. Some were no more than one room stacked above another with barely two strides from the porch to the gutter. Others had once been genteel, but the years had stripped their graces.

While Miranda dithered, Gideon was fast disappearing into the crowd. Gathering her courage, she dashed after him, dodging a wagon drawn by a dappled gray that reached out to nip her. Barely escaping its teeth, she dove into Maudlin's cool shadows where the leaning houses blocked the sunlight. Somewhere above, a raven squabbled with one of the tiny dragons that haunted the rooftops like living gargoyles. One or the other must have caught a rat, and she fervently hoped it wouldn't come tumbling out of the sky.

The street was crowded with peddlers, but not the kind who worked nicer streets. They stared at Miranda, clearly thinking her a lamb ripe for fleecing. She gave them a bland smile and kept going, wishing she'd brought a pistol.

Ahead, Wilcox and Gideon stopped before the only house that looked cared for, with glass in the windows and fresh paint on the trim. Reassured, Miranda sped up, her heels tap-tapping on the filthy cobbles. On the front steps of the house, Wilcox talked to an elegant woman while the messenger boy looked on.

Miranda reached Gideon's side, panting but doing her best to hide it.

Her brother scowled. "You couldn't resist, could you?"

"You're keeping secrets," she returned. "That's an outright challenge."

He made a noise of disgust. "Sometimes, there is a good reason for discretion."

"Why? Have you been here before?"

His expression turned scathing. "This is Hellion House."

The name made her start. Even she knew of the celebrated brothel. "Oh."

"Indeed."

Gideon shifted away from her, no doubt thinking he'd slammed the lid on her questions. Naturally, he was wrong.

"Who is that woman?" she asked.

"Mrs. Gillian Randall, the owner of the establishment."

She watched him from the corner of her eye. "How do you know that?"

"The good doctor knows her through his clinic."

That made sense. While Dr. Wilcox had a profitable medical practice, he opened his surgery to charity cases on two after-noons a week. This was probably how the doctor had met the occupants of Hellion House, which would explain why they'd sent for him today.

That didn't explain how Gideon knew this place, but she ran out of time to ponder. Mrs. Randall pointed to the side of the house and Wilcox ran down the porch steps, registering Miranda's presence with a lift of his brows.

"In the alley," he called, beckoning to Gideon.

The messenger boy ran ahead, leading the way into a narrow passage between Hellion House and its crumbling neighbor. A few feet inside the mouth of the passage, the child stopped, his face pale beneath its mask of dirt. When the men pushed forward into the shadows, Miranda followed, though the passageway was little more than an open sewer. Miranda lifted her skirts, gingerly picking her way around refuse.

Wilcox was farther ahead, crouching over a man who lay sprawled on his face. Gideon moved to block her view, but not before she saw blood pooling across the filth. The doctor already had his bag open, searching inside for supplies. The stark reality of the scene shocked her into action.

She pushed past her brother. "Let me help. I know how to bind an injury."

Gideon opened his mouth, but there was no objection he could make. Field medicine was part of her training with the Fletcher fleet, and she excelled at it.

"He's alive," Wilcox said, flipping the man over as she drew near.

The patient's coat was in tatters, and there were angry red welts covering his face and every other bit of exposed skin. Miranda had never seen anything like it.

"Where is the blood coming from?" she asked.

"His stomach." Wilcox parted the man's frock coat.

Miranda stifled a gasp. Something had ripped the man's soft belly with—she actually wasn't sure what would cause that kind of horrific damage. It looked as if a chunk of him was missing and the rest was about to spill out. Cold sweat coursed down Miranda's spine, and she swallowed hard. The gaping wound stank of bile and half-digested food. Jittering horror rose like a tide through her entire form.

Stop. Miranda stilled her thoughts, focusing on the problem in front of her. The man was breathing, if barely, and was mercifully unconscious.

"What do you need me to do?" she asked, heedless of her skirts as she knelt beside the man.

"Do you know how to take a pulse?" Dr. Wilcox asked.

"Certainly."

"Good. I need to know if it changes. And please be ready to hand me supplies from my bag."

She stripped off her gloves and found the man's pulse. His skin was cool and clammy. She counted beats, narrowing her attention until there was nothing but the patient and his needs.

Miranda glanced up only once as Gideon's footsteps scuffed behind her. He prowled up and down, alternately scanning the ground at his feet and the shadows lurking deeper down the passage. Was he searching for clues or standing guard? Miranda's skin chilled as it suddenly occurred to her the attacker might still be nearby.

"I've done what I can here," Wilcox said. "Help me move him inside."

Miranda stood back as Gideon took the man's feet. As she picked up the doctor's bag, she noticed a low-crowned hat rolling in the breeze, its brim crushed. The style was favored by businessmen and lawyers, and it almost certainly belonged to their patient. He'd had an ordinary life before he'd taken an unlucky shortcut down this passageway.

Subdued, Miranda followed Gideon and the doctor as they carried the unconscious man out to the street. Moments later, Mrs. Randall held the door to Hellion House open.

"Put him in the chamber beside the salon," she said. "It will be easier to tend him there."

Miranda finally saw the woman up close. She appeared to be in her mid-thirties, with her red hair pinned up in an ivory comb. Her butter-yellow day dress was trimmed with narrow rows of Gallic lace—tasteful rather than extravagant. Miranda grudgingly approved. Their gazes met, both women cautious.

"Your maid will probably quit when she sees those blood-stains," Mrs. Randall said.

The light comment caught Miranda off guard, but she heard the crack in the woman's voice. Like Miranda, she was putting on a brave face.

They both regarded at the ruins of Miranda's skirts. The pale fawn color hid nothing, and Shore would need every trick she knew to get the garment clean again. "I'll try bribery."

"A reasonable choice." Mrs. Randall retreated inside, word-lessly inviting Miranda in.

Miranda was all too aware that women of her class didn't enter brothels, but these were exceptional circumstances. She hurried to catch up to the others, unable to stifle her curiosity. The place appeared no different from any other house, at least in this public area. The only nod to the dwelling's purpose was a lamp on the newel post of the staircase. The brass base was a nymph in the grasp of a satyr, and they were obviously having a lovely time.

They reached their destination and lowered the man to a red velvet daybed. Wilcox addressed Miranda, his dark face solemn. "Help me cut his coat off."

She obeyed at once, retrieving shears from the doctor's bag. Once the jacket was off, she began working on his silk-lined waistcoat with not-quite-steady hands. After that came his blood-soaked shirt.

Now she could see the smaller wounds up close. Some were long scores, as if he'd wrestled with an enormous cat. Others were half-circles turning a puffed and weeping red. Miranda dropped the remains of the waistcoat to the floor, lightheaded with disbelief. *This man is covered in bite marks.*

"What happened to him?" she demanded, looking from the doctor to Gideon to Mrs. Randall, who stood by the door with a vertical crease between her fine brows. All were pale with shock, but none seemed surprised. Miranda felt queasy, as if she might lose the meal Gideon had bought her. "This isn't the first attack, is it?"

"Don't tell anyone you've seen this," Gideon said into the sudden silence. So, this was the secret he and Wilcox had been keeping.

She nodded slowly, aware this was dangerous information but not yet certain what it meant.

"He was with us at his usual time," the madam said in a low, musical voice. "He left under an hour ago. Layla heard his screams, and we went outside to see what the matter was. Perhaps the commotion scared his attacker away, but we found him alone and summoned help at once. He was just as you found him."

"You did not try to move him?" Wilcox asked. He his examination as he spoke.

"Not once we saw the extent of the injury," Mrs. Randall replied. "We feared making it worse, so we waited for you."

"Who is he?" Gideon asked.

"He told us his name is Tupper, but I don't know if he was telling the truth."

Mrs. Randall gave a wry smile. Of course, men who visited a brothel might lie.

Wilcox cursed under his breath. "He needs surgery."

"I can summon transport," Gideon offered.

"He's too weak to move again." The doctor frowned. "Bring hot water and clean towels. As many as you can. And more light."

"Already sent for," Mrs. Randall said.

As if by magic, a young woman appeared at the door, bearing a basin and towels. Miranda had half-expected the ladies of Hellion House to wear ostrich feathers and little else, but she'd been sorely mistaken. This female was dressed like one of the airfield's mechanics, a greasy smudge on her cheekbone. She set the hot water down on a table near Miranda and backed away, eyeing the wounded man with fascinated horror. Tupper was beginning to wake up. Soft sounds of distress hitched in his throat as his eyelids flickered.

Gideon leaned close. "Can you tell us what happened?"

Tupper didn't reply, seeming to sink back into his stupor. Anxious for some way to help, Miranda soaked one of the towels in water and began to wipe the blood from his face. Tupper gave a startled exclamation, as if even her light touch caused him pain.

"What attacked you?" Gideon asked.

Tupper's eyes flew open, terror making a mask of his features. He took in a stuttering breath, and Miranda thought he would answer, but then he seemed to choke. Wilcox shouldered Gideon aside, checking the man's airway and pressing an ear to his chest. Tupper's hand flexed into a fist, rising as if to fend off a remembered blow, then fell limply at his side. A final gasp left his throat.

Wilcox straightened, shaking his head.

Shock numbed Miranda, making the silence ring in her head. She dropped the towel beside the basin of water, then blindly began washing her hands, tears stinging her eyes. It seemed disrespectful to wash Tupper's life blood away as if it were filthy, yet a scream worked its way up her throat at the sticky, intimate feel.

"What in the name of all the gods tears a man open that way?" Mrs. Randall asked, her voice shaking. "It was outside my house in broad daylight."

"Not daylight," a new voice said. "Not really."

They all spun, toward the passageway outside the door. The man who entered wore no uniform, but he held up the badge of a police inspector. "Not daylight," he repeated. "It is dark as Hades in that alleyway."

"Detective Inspector Palmer," Mrs. Randall said, suddenly cool.

"I come in peace," Palmer stated with an ironic twist of his lips. He was fair-haired and lean, with the hollow look of someone who hadn't slept for a dozen nights. "My inquiry does not concern your house today."

"And yet, you are in it," Mrs. Randall said dryly.

"Only because a man was done for in the alley." Palmer took out a cigarette case, read her expression, then returned it to his pocket.

"This tragedy just happened," she said. "How did you know about it so quickly?"

"I have ears on the ground." Palmer scanned the room, deep brown eyes seeming to miss nothing. "Ones I pay for information."

"You mean Billy," said Gideon.

For the first time, Miranda realized the boy was missing, and had been since they'd found Tupper.

"The lad knows his business. More to the point, he knows mine." Palmer lifted the bloody waistcoat from the floor. "This isn't the first attack of this kind."

"How many do you know of?" Gideon asked.

"Several." Gingerly, Palmer extracted a gold watch from the waistcoat's pocket. "And none were robberies."

Then why had they happened? Miranda's gaze flew to Tupper's motionless form. There had been no time to cover him up, and the man seemed achingly vulnerable.

Palmer turned the watch over, perhaps looking for an inscription. "Do we know this gentleman's name?"

Miranda opened her mouth to speak, but Gideon jumped in, as if to keep her from Palmer's notice. "He gave his name as Tupper. The attack occurred about an hour ago."

The inspector pulled out a notebook, then began jotting down the offered details.

"We know there were other deaths," Gideon replied, glancing to where Wilcox stood by the window. "The doctor has examined two victims before this."

"I'm well familiar with Dr. Wilcox and his work in the community," Palmer said. "But who are you?"

"Gideon Fletcher."

"The heir to the airships," Palmer said. "I'm honored. And who is the young lady covered in Mr. Tupper's blood?"

"My sister. She is here strictly by chance. She tried to help."

"Of course," Palmer said in a kinder voice than he'd used so far. "And if she is present, I assume you were not here in a recreational capacity?"

"No."

"Then what's your involvement?"

Miranda stopped breathing. That was exactly what she wanted to know.

"Stop talking," Dr. Wilcox broke in. He was gazing out the window, his shoulders hunched.

"What is it?" Palmer asked.

The doctor turned to face them, his face tight with anxiety. "The Conclave is here."

CHAPTER 5

Gideon stiffened. "Who tipped them off?"

"Billy," Mrs. Randall and Palmer said at once, their eyes meeting.

"The lad will do anything for a coin," Palmer added.

"Do you recognize anyone?" Gideon asked.

"Councilor Ormond," Wilcox replied.

Miranda knew nothing of the man, but she read her brother's reaction. It wasn't good. Her heartbeat quickened. "What do we do?"

"What can we do?" Wilcox asked unhappily.

Silence fell. Miranda heard the carriage door slam, then the murmur of voices outside.

"Go," Palmer said to Gideon. "I'm afraid the doctor's presence is necessary, but you two are not. Escort your sister out of here. I'll find you if I have more questions."

"Thank you," Miranda said, though Palmer did not look up from his notes.

Gideon wasted no time. "Where is your back entrance?" he asked Mrs. Randall.

She gave a slight smile. "Don't go out the back. It's too obvious. Go upstairs."

Gideon took Miranda's arm, hurriedly escorting her out of the room. As little as she liked being pulled along, she obeyed without argument. Mrs. Randall followed them to the main part of Hellion House.

"Janey," Mrs. Randall called. "Janey, where are you? Show our guests out by the upstairs route."

The girl dressed in overalls sauntered out from a side room. "We'll use the servants' stairs," she said, pointing a thumb over her shoulder. "It's the best way to keep out of sight."

They could hear heavy footfalls on the front steps—at least four or five pairs of feet. Surprise crossed Janey's face, and she led them into the kitchen at a trot, shutting the door once they were through. A hard rap echoed through the house.

"Who's that?" the girl asked.

"A problem," Gideon replied. "We need to hurry."

Miranda hugged herself, her breath coming quick and fast. The kitchen was neat and well-stocked, but the orderly calm did nothing to soothe her. She might be adventurous, but this kind of risk was new.

Janey herded them to the narrow stairs at the rear of the room. "Careful, these squeak." She went up first, her blond braid swinging like a pendulum down her back.

Miranda followed on tiptoe, with Gideon behind her. Like all servants' stairs, these wound through the workaday parts of the house. Flight after flight, the steps grew narrower as they rose, finally reaching a door at the top landing. Janey opened it with a key fastened to her belt by a chain.

They exited onto the flat roof, sending a crow flapping away with an indignant squawk. Like every home in Londria, this place had a rooftop garden. It was small—just a few planters of carrots and cabbages—but it was served by one of the aqueducts that delivered water to the city's many sky gardens. Inside the walls, people made use of whatever space they could find to grow food.

Janey held a finger to her lips. It was easy to guess why—sound carried. Palmer and the madam must have been on the front porch, because their words were crystal clear.

"There should be some attempt to locate the man's family," Mrs. Randall said. "They should have the opportunity to give him a decent burial."

"Sadly, we must take his remains to the Citadel," said a voice. By the note of authority, Miranda guessed it belonged to Councilor Ormond.

A tense silence followed, but Palmer eventually broke it. "Why the rush to take him? I haven't begun my investigation into his murder."

"There's no hope of solving a crime committed on this derelict street. Should you even find a witness, there is no guarantee they were sober and in their right mind."

"Again, what of his family?" Mrs. Randall asked, her tone cold as ice.

"We are sparing them the humiliation of finding their loved one in this disreputable establishment."

"Why are you involved?" asked Palmer.

Gideon and Miranda exchanged a glance. *An excellent question.*

"Please stand aside, Detective Inspector Palmer," Ormond said, his voice void of any feeling. "And you, too, Madam."

"I protest," Mrs. Randall said, equally cool.

"How unfortunate. You should be grateful we are removing his remains at no expense to your business."

There was the sound of shuffling feet. The next words came from a different man—most likely one of the Conclave guards. "Search the house. Spare nothing."

Janey's breath hissed out in alarm.

"Go," the young woman said, urgent now. "Go to the next

building. Watch for rotting spots on the roof. Use the aqueducts where you can. There are stairs by the bridge."

With that, she sprinted back through the stairwell door.

"Why search the house?" Miranda whispered. "Do they think Tupper hid something here?"

"I doubt it. They wish to show they are in charge." Gideon grabbed Miranda's hand, and they quickly crossed the flat surface of the roof. He pulled her into a crouch by the edge. "Can you run in those clothes?"

"Of course." Miranda checked to ensure her hat was firmly pinned, then stuffed her reticule inside her coat to free her hands. "I always keep up."

"Indeed, you do," Gideon replied with no little sarcasm. "Whether it's good for you or not."

"Be grateful," she returned tartly. "If I wasn't here, Palmer might have kept you downstairs."

Gideon did not look impressed, so she let the matter drop.

The building next door was shorter, with no rooftop garden. That meant it lacked a convenient connection via the aqueduct. In fact, the place seemed abandoned—which explained Janey's comment about rotten spots in the roof.

"How do you suggest we get down there?" Miranda asked.

The sound of glass breaking on the floor below was loud—no doubt the guards conducting their so-called search.

"Quickly," Gideon answered. "Can you make the jump?"

She made a scoffing noise. "That's not a jump; it's a long step."

That wasn't exactly true. The gap was easily five feet across with a drop equal to a man's height. Her head felt suddenly light. It *would* be easier if she were wearing her airman's uniform, but she'd just have to manage.

Gideon's mouth clamped in a thin line. He went first, leaping across the distance. She watched him land in a roll, then jump lightly to his feet. Once settled, he held out his arms to catch her.

Miranda made the mistake of looking down. Four stories below, the bright eyes of scavenging dragons peered up from the refuse. She caught a glimpse of Mrs. Randall on the street flanked by Conclave guards in their red-and-gold uniforms. The woman's head was high, her fists in angry balls. Everything about her posture said someone would pay.

Another window broke. Miranda had to jump *now*. Heart in her mouth, she backed up, took a few running steps, then leaped with her skirts billowing around her. Gideon caught her, swinging her around so her boots landed firmly on the sagging roof.

"Run," he said.

She did, alert to the slightest crunch that warned the structure wouldn't take her weight. It was Gideon who nearly lost a shoe when his heel punched through the surface, but they made it to the other side.

Miranda heard the rooftop door of Hellion House slam open. She grabbed Gideon's sleeve, pulling him down behind the big square chimney of the derelict house. Voices floated on the breeze as the guards searched, but they were too far away to make out the words. She hoped Dr. Wilcox was all right.

"Why do you think Palmer let us go?" Miranda whispered.

"We're rich," Gideon replied. "He's not. We'll be hearing from him the next time he needs a favor."

"That's cynical."

"It's either that or he's an altruist. Which do you think is more plausible?"

Miranda digested his theory. It wasn't a pretty explanation, but it was a likely one.

She moved on. "Why does the Conclave want Tupper's body?"

"I don't know for sure."

"Have they taken the bodies from all the attacks?"

"I suspect they do when they know about it." Gideon stared

out at the skyline. "I don't intend to tell them I've seen other victims. They seem to disapprove of witnesses."

As if to underscore his point, another window smashed.

"What's our next move?" she asked.

"The aqueduct. It's three feet from the corner of the roof. Just a short step this time," he added with a big-brother smile that made her grind her teeth. "Then we walk to the bridge."

"That's half a mile, at least."

"Too much?"

"No." *Yes.* She was used to going distances of a dozen yards or so on the narrow brick structures. Most were about a foot and a half wide—enough room to balance, but the walkways were three and four stories above the ground, and none had handrails. She closed her eyes, breathing deeply to calm her racing pulse.

Eventually, the rooftop door slammed again. Miranda opened her eyes again and peered around the corner of the chimney. Dusk was creeping into the sky, and the rooftop of Hellion House was empty. "They've gone."

Gideon got to his feet, then helped her up. "Let's go before we lose the light."

"Wait a moment," Miranda said. "One thing I must say before we go. Whatever I just said about Palmer letting us go, I know you would rather have stayed to see what you could find out."

He shrugged. "And have another charming conversation with Councilor Ormond? Trust me, I'm happy to be dancing on rooftops right now."

"I'm being serious."

"So am I," he replied.

"Then tell me why you went with Dr. Wilcox," she said. "You must have known what you'd find."

"I needed to see one more victim to confirm what I've been thinking. Now I have."

"And?"

"I've seen bites like that before."

A tiny suspicion niggled in the back of her mind. "Where?"

"Mostly in the forest."

The penny dropped. "That's why you're searching for a breach in the barrier."

"The Conclave is lying," he said. "The Unseen are inside the city. The barrier can't keep us safe anymore."

CHAPTER 6

"Why in the name of all that is holy did you drag your sister over miles of treacherous brickwork in the dark?" asked Fletcher.

It was later the same night, and Gideon was in his father's study. Miranda had retired, but he had been summoned like a tardy pupil to the headmaster's office. By the open ledger and stack of correspondence on the desk, Gideon guessed his father had been reviewing the business accounts.

"You're exaggerating," Gideon said calmly, settling into an armchair on the other side of the desk.

Glowering, Fletcher crumpled the paper he held into a ball. Then, seeming surprised by his action, proceeded to smooth it out again, muttering curses all the while. Gideon recognized the document as an invoice from one of their usual suppliers.

"I'm not exaggerating by much." His father's voice had grown dangerously quiet. "I will put up with your fits and starts of behavior because you are my son—and because I respect a man's right to his own ideas, within reason. I will not tolerate you putting my girls into danger."

Fletcher's voice was rising now, taking on the snap of a captain

"

disciplining his crew. "It was bad enough you risked Miranda's reputation by taking her to a bookstore in that neighborhood, to say nothing of Hellion House. What were you thinking, boy?"

"We made it safely home." Even as Gideon said it, he knew they'd been lucky. Cold and fatigue had taken a toll on them both, but it was nothing a night of sleep wouldn't cure.

"The fact that you made it home doesn't excuse what happened," Fletcher said darkly. "I thought you had better judgment."

"Miranda will demand to see more of the world," Gideon replied. "It's in her nature. I would rather be there to guide her than have her indulge her curiosity on her own."

"What do you know of raising daughters?" his father snapped. "What would you have done if she'd landed in real trouble?"

I would have shown her how to save herself. Gideon reclined in his chair, careful to keep his tongue in check. If Miranda shared his taste for adventure, Fletcher shared his temper.

Gideon looked away, surveying the familiar room so he didn't have to meet his father's glare. The study reflected Fletcher's personality. The room was spartan, devoid of the plush comforts found in every other part of Allington House. There were cubby holes filled with rolls of plans, a desk and a worktable, and sketches of airships pinned to the walls. There was no pretense here, nothing claiming Norton Fletcher was anything but a plain-spoken, hardworking man. The levelheaded humility made Gideon respect his father as no fortune or title ever would. But respect didn't mean harmony between father and son.

"I regret—" Gideon began.

"Don't." Fletcher pointed a forefinger. "We've gone beyond regret, my boy. You dragged Miranda into a regrettable situation —a murder, no less."

"Hang on—"

"*And then,* you actually fled over the rooftops from an infamous brothel to escape our old friend Councilor Ormond. *What if he had caught her?"*

Gideon flinched. "I didn't mean for the situation to become dire."

"You are a fool." Fletcher's face flushed crimson. "You had no right to risk her safety."

"Perhaps." It had seemed natural to take Miranda into his confidence, even if it only meant escorting her to meet Dobson. She was the one sibling who shared his depthless curiosity. "As I tried to say, I regret how things turned out."

Fletcher's chair creaked as he shifted his weight, obviously trying to ease a spine made stiff by half a century of building engines. "Don't fill her head her with notions of adventure."

And that was where Fletcher failed to understand his daughters at all. "Constraint is what makes her unhappy. She's not a natural hostess, like Sidonie. Nor is she an academic, like Olivia. Miranda needs her freedom."

Fletcher grunted. "You might want to examine Londria's underbelly, but keep her out of it. More to the point, don't draw her to the Conclave's notice."

"She wants to know the truth as much as I do."

"What truth?"

"But that's the point." The conversation had finally circled to where Gideon wanted it—to talk about what he'd found out. "There is something loose in the city the Conclave doesn't want discovered. It would prove they are not the omnipotent fathers of the city as they'd have us believe."

"Nonsense." Fletcher heaved a sigh. "You saw Ormond fix the barrier. The Conclave can make repairs in the time it takes us to dress for dinner."

"If they know about a breach, that is. What if they didn't?"

"We'd be dead in our beds by now," Fletcher said firmly.

"Would we?" Gideon mused. "Ormond said it himself. The

forest isn't the only home to hungry creatures. The city could be, too."

"Then why aren't more people dead?"

"We've always assumed a breach would lead to a massacre. What if the Unseen hunt one meal at a time? Who would miss a lone beggar from the slums, or even a good citizen who vanishes without a trace?" Gideon's blood ran cold. He rose to pace, hoping movement would shake off memories of Tupper's death. "We blame ruffians and footpads, but what if the cause is something else?"

His father chuckled. "That's an old myth drummed up to scare the rabble."

Gideon wheeled. "Why won't you consider what I have to say?"

Fletcher rose stiffly and crossed to the plans table, pushing aside the scatter of drawings until he uncovered a tray with a decanter and glasses. The crystal was old and chipped—his father rarely threw anything out—but the brandy was excellent. He poured two glasses, then handed one to his son. "Let's look at this logically, then put it to bed."

"Thank you."

"What you say is not impossible," Fletcher admitted. "I don't know history, but I do know how building projects work. The Great Disaster forced humanity to move out of the countryside and behind walls, but that did not happen overnight. The barrier is a hodge-podge of construction, each section built when and where folks saw the need. Gaps occur when an object is stitched together after the fact. Inevitably, there are engineering flaws."

"Exactly," Gideon replied.

"But here's the problem. The protection doesn't come from the bricks and mortar—it comes from the magic."

Gideon warmed the brandy glass in his hand, but he was too absorbed in the conversation to taste it. "What about the barrier spell? Was it made all at once or here and there, like the wall itself?"

"Who knows?" Fletcher tossed back his drink. "No one kept records back then—at least none you and I will ever see. But we both witnessed how the barrier threw the monsters off our wall, and that's evidence enough for me."

"But I'm telling you the barrier isn't perfect. Something is getting through. There's a police inspector investigating the same series of deaths Wilcox noticed."

"The plods are useful for catching pickpockets, but this is beyond them."

A headache began to pound behind Gideon's right eye. "Then what do you think is ripping the guts out of ordinary citizens?"

"Dogs? An ambitious dragon? Forget theories—I'll give you facts. After the Great Disaster, the Citadel, the new roads, and the barrier had to be built piece by piece. The Conclave accomplished all of that, and they did it while the city was under attack."

"I'm not questioning the fact it was a huge undertaking."

"But you are. You're looking for flaws in a system that's kept us safe for centuries. I dislike the Citadel and its laws. Councilors like Ormond are proud, sometimes cruel men. But we are indebted to the mages because their work saves our lives every hour of every day."

Gideon bridled. If Black's life had fueled a single repair, then how many innocent lives had it cost to cast a shield around the whole city? "The Conclave's protection comes at a price."

"Everything does." Fletcher's tone was flat. "If you think otherwise, you're an utter dolt. Even if it's imperfect and there *are* monsters under our beds, it's still a bargain if most of us are safe."

"But what if that could change?" Gideon set his glass down harder than he meant to.

His father slowly shook his head. "You have a great deal to learn, my boy. You shot a man, and you're understandably upset.

But Black was not the first or last to sacrifice his life for this city's safety. Soldiers die, son. Magic has nothing to do with it."

Gideon's face went numb with anger. "Did he need to make that sacrifice? Will anyone else?"

"What's the alternative?"

"What if the Great Disaster could be undone?"

There, he had said it. The one dream he'd never heard proposed because it would make the Conclave useless.

Fletcher's eyebrows dipped. "Do you mean to send the creatures in the forest back to where they came from? That's... imaginative."

"Ideas start somewhere. If no one speaks the words, it will never happen."

Fletcher stared at his son for a long moment, a flicker of hope darkening to bitterness in his eyes. He slammed his glass on the worktable, making the last drops of brandy jump and splatter. "Forget fairy tales and stop spouting nonsense. Your concern should be for the family's future. You belong to Fletcher Industries."

Fletcher's tone momentarily stunned him. Gideon might as well have run headlong into a brick wall. "I'm not you."

"You are my heir, and you're courting a charge of treason. Do me the courtesy of inheriting my life's work before you piss it into the gutter." Fletcher was flushed, the veins in his neck pulsing against the white of his collar.

Sweat trickled between Gideon's shoulder blades. "*You* just admitted the barrier could be fallible. *You* taught me the search for improvement is the only impulse that truly keeps a business alive. Should the city do less? Shouldn't we walk beyond the wall as free men and women, without fear of tyrants and monsters?"

"You sound like a madman preaching on the street corners." Fletcher curled his lip as he flung himself into the chair behind the desk.

Anger darkened the edges of Gideon's vision. Sarcasm meant real communication had ended. "You're afraid."

Fletcher's head snapped up, eyes dark with anger. "I bloody am, you lumbering fool. If Ormond heard you now, you'd end up in the Citadel like Joseph Ellery, never to be seen again." Fletcher panted slightly, as if squashing Gideon's argument took physical force.

"Father—" Gideon began in worry, but Fletcher cut him off with a slice of his hand through the air.

"Think what twaddle you like, but keep your mouth shut and your head down outside this room. Think of your sisters. I have few rules in this family, but self-preservation—the *family's* preservation—is at the top of the list."

"I should forget what I saw with my own eyes today?"

"Didn't the Conclave come to fetch the body? What does that tell you?" His father pounded a forefinger on the desk. "Pursuing the matter is dangerous folly."

With that, he picked up a pencil and began ticking off numbers on the invoice he'd crumpled before. Dumb with resentment, Gideon turned on his heel and marched to the door.

His father said nothing, refusing to continue the fight.

Gideon's hand rested on the doorknob, wondering what else there was to say or if his father would call him back. The struggle to obey—or not to obey—after years of hero-worship was hard.

Nothing came but the scratch of Fletcher's pencil.

"I'm going to see Wilcox," Gideon said. "I want to ensure he made it home safely."

I must find out what happened after we left.

His father—never a fool—had to understand the subtext. There were still questions to ask, and Gideon wouldn't let them go.

Fletcher didn't reply.

The silence too loud to bear, Gideon left the room.

CHAPTER 7

The next morning found Miranda on the roof of Allington House. She wore one of her oldest dresses, a comfortable gown that was threadbare at the hem but easy to move around in. The raised beds of the garden spread around her, yellowing leaves rustling in the cool October breeze. Most everything but the root vegetables had faded, but it still made for a pleasant place to practice with her bow and arrow. Normally, she would have gone to the airfield. Today, however, she sensed her father would be happier if she stayed close to home.

She drew the recurved bow, stilled her churning thoughts, and released the arrow. It flew with a hum of feathers to land with a thump two circles outside the bull's-eye. Close, but not close enough for Miranda's liking.

The target was set at the other end of the expansive roof. She was skilled enough there was no real chance of stray arrows. Even so, she'd had a footman pile bales of straw behind and around the target just in case.

Miranda plucked another arrow from the row she'd planted in the carrot bed like a strange feathered crop. The tame dragonets in the aviary next door squawked for attention, but she refused to let them out of the cage, afraid they'd accidentally get in the way. Besides, she needed this time to ponder, even though it was hard to do with the beastly things mugging for a scratch behind their adorably pointed ears.

Gwennie Prasad, the neighbor's child who raised the pets, held a special place in Miranda's heart. Alongside Gwennie were other irreplaceable treasures, like afternoon croquet with her sisters and the way her father buttered his toast with the precision of a mason spreading mortar. There had been afternoons reading to her mother before poems had lost their charm for the dying woman, and the last gentle word before she'd left this earth.

As much as they gave her comfort, the memories didn't belong in the same universe as yesterday's horrors. Miranda had experienced fear before, but she'd never come this close to evil's handiwork. The sight of Tupper's torn body had wounded her in a way she could not define. That blow had been compounded by the sound of the Conclave guards smashing the windows of Hellion House. Miranda hadn't known witnessing such acts could change her, but they had, Rage left her feeling ill and unclean.

She drew the bow again, conjuring a figure wearing the uniform of a Conclave guard. The arrow flew. This time, it hit dead center. A spike of satisfaction coursed through her as she lowered the bow. No, she didn't feel *unclean*, exactly. She was resentful, because she was forced to guard the softer place inside herself like an oyster closing around its pearl. The powers that allowed these terrible acts were forcing her to hide.

Miranda ran through the rest of the arrows, but there were no more bull's-eyes. Annoyed, she retrieved her equipment and unstrung her bow. Her arms were tired, and she wanted a cup of tea. Picking up her gear, she blew a kiss to the dragonets and went inside to call her maid. It was time to dress for luncheon.

"Good practice, miss?" asked the young footman who took her bow and quiver as she passed him in the corridor.

"Excellent, Stanley. The breeze was in my favor."

"Glad to hear it, miss."

He grinned, a thousand quips about Cupid lurking in his smile. Miranda walked away before he could utter a single one—not that a proper servant would.

Although she'd always kept up her archery, Miranda preferred the firearms training at the airfield. Though Fletcher Industries didn't train its airmen as soldiers, good marksmanship was essential for flights over the monster-infested forests.

She enjoyed the physical exercise and fresh air, not to mention the sense of control that daily practice gave her. She'd even tried some of the specialized aether guns guaranteed to down an Unseen with a single shot, but they were unstable and woefully clumsy for someone of her slight build.

In a fit of irritation, she'd once sketched a weapon suitable for a smaller hand, but she didn't have her father's skill to actually build it—and there was no point in asking for his help. While Miranda could train with a crew—and was as good a shot as Gideon—her father would never allow her to fly over the wall as anything but a well-guarded passenger.

To put it another way, it would be a rare day that Miranda actually *needed* an aether gun. Then again, given Tupper's murder, should she try harder to find a gunsmith?

There was a letter waiting on her dressing table, no doubt placed there by the housemaid. Curious, Miranda picked it up, feeling the weight of the expensive cream paper. It was addressed in a woman's elegant handwriting. It had no return address, nor did the seal bear a crest. She broke the wax and unfolded the note, catching the scent of amber perfume. A single line was written in violet ink.

Meet me at the Mercury Café at one o'clock.

Miranda sniffed. Only a very silly person would rush to a

secret rendezvous with an unknown correspondent. Such things inevitably ended in scandal.

She folded the note before stuffing it in her drawer.

What kind of scandal could it possibly be?

She took the note out again to examine the paper for clues. Miranda's lips parted in surprise when she saw the watermark belonged to a continental stationer. Who got writing paper flown in from over the sea? Someone with important connections. That much was certain.

Miranda searched for other clues, but there was nothing to find. Disappointed, she began to fold the page again. What had Dobson said? *Sometimes, a person has to make an effort to get answers.*

She'd never been to the Mercury Café, but she had a general idea of where it was located. The café sat on a shabby street fashionable with the university set.

Miranda glanced at the ormolu timepiece ticking quietly on the bookshelf. One o'clock wasn't far off.

If she hurried, she could make it.

She chose a dress she could put on without the aid of her maidservant—a walking dress with black-and-pink stripes decorated with elaborate frogging. Miranda put on a straw hat with a black lace veil, fixing it with a long hat pin, and then slipped her smallest pistol into her reticule. Both the pin and the pistol were effective weapons, and the veil would allow her to assess the environment without being recognized. Adventure was one thing, but she was not going to rush blindly forward. Yesterday had taught her that lesson.

Minutes later, the coachman handed her into the family's curricle. Young ladies typically traveled with their maids in tow, but hers was a gossip. Jackson, however, had been with the Fletchers as long as Miranda could remember. He had always kept her secrets.

Once they'd reached the approximate destination, she had

him pull up and wait a few doors away. She wanted to slip into the café without drawing attention, and the vehicle stood out in the Bohemian neighborhood.

"Are you certain about this, miss?" Jackson asked, his weathered face creased with concern.

"I'm entering a public eatery, nothing more," Miranda replied. "Reason says the greatest danger will be dribbling coffee on my new skirt."

"If you don't mind my saying, miss, reason isn't the same as instinct. What does your stomach tell you?"

"That if I'm not back in half an hour, please come find me," she said, lowering the veil on her hat.

"Yes, Miss Miranda," Jackson said, lowering the steps of the vehicle so she could make her descent. "Will I need a horse whip or a pistol when I come to fetch you?"

"I leave that to your judgment," she said brightly. "I'm hopeful basic fisticuffs will suffice."

"Right you are, miss," Jackson said with a bow.

Miranda set out, determined not to be nervous. She knew immediately which establishment she wanted. The café had large blue awnings that stretched across the width of the building. Bicycles leaned against the front wall, evidence of local students.

As soon as she went inside, she saw most of the patrons were her age, dressed in the colorful fashions of the university crowd. Gaggles of them crowded around bare wooden tables, voices raised in loud conversation. Others sat on stools at a long bar, where they could drink and read the newspaper in peace. Along the edges of the room, a few women, like her, wore heavy veils. Evidently, this was a popular place to meet incognito.

Miranda threaded her way between the tables, the scent of spicy soup and fresh bread making her mouth water. Steam-powered carafes dispensed tiny cups of thick black coffee amid clouds of vapor. At the back, a glass counter held trays of cakes rotating on clockwork stands. Her stomach rumbled—she hadn't yet had her midday meal—but she wasn't there to eat. She scanned the tables in search of a familiar face.

Mrs. Randall sat alone at a table, far away from the front window. Dressed in a deep blue ensemble, the woman's coppery hair was upswept and topped by a black straw hat adorned with a jaunty feather. She was the last person Miranda had expected to see, but she was the only one there Miranda knew. She had to be the anonymous correspondent.

For a moment, Miranda considered leaving. If anyone saw them together, her reputation would be compromised—and yet could she really walk away without learning what the woman had to say? Miranda crossed the restaurant and sat, curiosity at a boil.

Mrs. Randall studied Miranda through the veil. This close, the lace netting provided less anonymity.

"Thank you for meeting me, Miss Fletcher," she said quietly. "I wasn't sure you would respond."

Miranda straightened. "How could I resist?"

"You might have. People choose to ignore a great many things."

One of the servers arrived, sporting a waxed moustache that stuck up like the hands of a clock about to strike two. "My ladies, what is your pleasure?"

"Just coffee, please, Ivan," Mrs. Randall said, then turned her gaze on Miranda. "Though I do recommend the pastries here. They are quite exquisite."

"Just tea with lemon, if you please."

The man gave a brisk nod before hurrying away.

Unsettled, Miranda got to the point. "Why did you ask me here?"

Mrs. Randall arched a brow at Miranda's directness. The woman was apparently prepared to be humble, but not humbled. "I contacted you for several reasons. First among is them is to compliment you on your presence of mind yesterday. You were impressive for a young woman of your experience."

"Thank you," Miranda said, not quite liking the *for your experience*, however justified. "Was everyone all right after we left?"

The corners of the woman's mouth pulled down. She had an elven face, the features heightened by a liveliness Miranda likened to a bird. Now, however, that energy turned brittle. "We gave them poor Tupper in the end, but they did considerable damage to prove they were in control of the situation. Fortunately, no one was injured."

"Are they going to search for Tupper's attacker?"

"Palmer will. For all he likes the sound of his own voice, he's good at his job. The others—I don't know."

"Who do you think killed Tupper?"

The question made the woman swallow, the muscles in her slender throat working nervously. "Who—or do you mean what? Tales of monsters have been growing like mold over a cheese these past months. Me, I prefer to believe monsters are the masks we give our own fears. At least, when we are in the city."

Miranda nodded. "But people have gone missing, or so I hear."

"People—especially young ones with money to spend—sometimes leave their homes without warning. Many fly to another city in search of novelty. Others unexpectedly join the Conclave, though I cannot fathom why."

"We all know someone like that," Miranda said.

"Of course. Vanishing doesn't mean they were eaten by dragons —no reasonable person would believe it. Until yesterday, that is. The moment I heard Tupper..." She trailed off, the color draining from her face. "Then those tall tales suddenly seemed real."

"Gideon says there have been other victims."

"He does."

"What did he tell you?"

"Not much." Mrs. Randall's expression shifted to amusement.

"I am not his confidante. He's simply a casual acquaintance, not a customer of the house."

Miranda's cheeks grew hot behind her veil. "Where did you meet?"

"Here." The woman swept the room with her gaze. "The Mercury is where makers and philosophers come to hear their dreams whisper. Your brother visits from time to time, as do I. It turns out we both enjoy a glass of absinthe."

Miranda sat back, unsure what to make of that. "So, you raised a drink and spoke of murders?"

Mrs. Randall gave a low chuckle. The conversation stopped while the server delivered their drinks. Miranda stirred her tea, not sure what to say next.

"No doubt you wonder why I wrote to ask you here," the woman said.

"Yes, naturally."

"I was asked to give you this." Mrs. Randall reached into her reticule, then extracted a slender book. She slid the tiny volume across the table. "It was left by a woman who stayed at Hellion House a few months ago. Her professional name is Madam Alma."

"The fortune teller?" Miranda straightened in her chair. "I met her."

Sidonie had hired Madam Alma to entertain at a party. It had been a risky move since any kind of magic outside the Conclave —even for entertainment—was strictly illegal. To make matters worse, the Conclave's guards had mounted a house-to-house search for unauthorized magic-users that very night. The three Fletcher sisters had hidden Madam Alma in the attic, both for her safety and theirs.

"From what she said," Mrs. Randall continued, "you had a hand in her escape from the city."

That was true. The last Miranda had seen of the woman, she'd been rowing down the river under the starlight. "You've seen her since? She's safe?"

"She spoke to me last night," Mrs. Randall replied, not quite answering the question. "She mentioned you were interested in her deck of tarot cards."

Madam Alma had actually gifted the deck to Miranda. She still had them concealed under the floorboards of her bedroom.

Mrs. Randall sipped her coffee. "She referred to you as the scorpion."

"That was the card I drew when she read my fortune."

Miranda picked up the book. The cover was so worn the title was illegible. She opened it to read the yellowed frontispiece, then closed it at once. It was a treatise on how to use the tarot— information the Conclave would definitely forbid if they knew about it. Her fingertips tingled, eager to turn the pages of cramped text. Instead, she slipped the book into her own reticule. "Thank you for delivering this."

"Alma said it was important you understand what the scorpion symbol means."

Miranda scanned the café, cautious of eavesdroppers. However subversive the patrons of the Mercury might be, the conversation had strayed to topics too dangerous for a public place. "She told me the scorpion is a protector."

"Do you know its legend?"

Miranda recalled Madam Alma's exact words. "When the great hunter Orion grew mad with bloodlust, the gods sent the humble scorpion to protect the land and its creatures. The scorpion was small and insignificant, so Orion did not guard himself against its sting. Thus, the hunter became the prey."

"And?"

The question hung in the air, but Miranda had no answers. In truth, the matter had given her many sleepless nights. What did it mean to be the scorpion? What was she supposed to do? She was an independent thinker with a good sense of style and a decent shot. It made her an interesting party guest, but not much else.

"And I should go," Miranda said with finality. "It's past time I returned home."

Mrs. Randall put a hand over hers. "One other thing, Miss Fletcher. Hellion House is more than it appears. Some of the women take gentleman callers, but only by choice. Others are makers like Janey or women like Alma, who are simply in need of a safe haven."

Miranda waited, wondering where the conversation was going.

"One person alone can't remake the world, but together our house has made a difference. If you ever need a place to retreat, my door is open to you."

"At Hellion House?" Miranda exclaimed, too surprised to stifle the words.

"I can see the invitation comes as a surprise," Mrs. Randall said, unruffled. "I hope for your sake that you never need to take advantage of the offer."

But even as the woman spoke, an idea took shape in Miranda's mind. "Did you say Janey is a maker?"

"I did."

"What does she know about firearms?"

CHAPTER 8

*D*isaster comes in many forms. In this case, it arrived by way of Olivia's dressmaker.

Olivia occupied the uncomfortable position of middle child in the Fletcher household, two years younger than Sidonie and Gideon, who were twins, and a year older than Miranda. A genius in mathematics, Olivia corresponded with celebrated professors about numbers that may or may not exist, or only existed under arcane conditions that boggled Miranda's mind. Sadly, little of Olivia's prowess translated to daily life.

"Look at these ruffles," Olivia demanded as she burst into Sidonie's bedroom, where Miranda was borrowing a pair of gloves. Both sisters turned to Olivia, who held out her arms like a soprano about to launch into an aria. "I look like a throw pillow."

Miranda bit her lip. Some people could not be trusted to visit the *modiste* alone.

The gown was pretty, the style taken from the latest fashion pages. But Mademoiselle Thibault should have known better than to cave to Olivia's choices. The soft pink satin and enthusiastic ruching did not flatter her angular frame. Where she could have been striking—even imposing—Olivia appeared to have been upholstered.

"Why do intelligent adults subject themselves to Society occasions?" Olivia complained. "It is a great deal of time and money thrown away just to be named in the gossip pages."

"Oh, come now," Sidonie said with a laugh. She was seated at her dressing table, trying on one pair of earrings after another. "If you had your way, Richard and I would elope and save you the inconvenience of attending a wedding."

"We do own a fleet of airships," Olivia said tartly. "It's still hours before the betrothal ball. You have time."

"Noted." Sidonie examined a pair of pearl drops. "Perhaps I shall wear these."

"I need to order something else." Olivia plucked at her sleeves. "This won't do."

"There's no time for a new dress," Sidonie stated.

"Don't be beastly. I know that."

"Wear your green gown. It looks lovely on you."

"People have seen it before."

"Better to be remembered for something perfect twice over than, well, that," Sidonie replied, growing impatient. "Really, Olivia, you should have addressed this weeks ago. Didn't you try it on?"

Remaining silent, Miranda let the other two spar as she examined her eldest sister's collection of gloves. It wasn't worth playing peacemaker. She'd learned—to her grief—that no one loved a neutral party. Interference meant incurring both her sisters' wrath.

And she'd had quite enough barbs from her family of late. Two days before, Papa had called her into his office for a word. Later, when comparing notes with Gideon, she learned they'd received similar lectures. Miranda was instructed to say nothing of what she'd seen and done at Hellion House, to clear her mind of questions, and to behave like a model lady.

Her father's orders chafed. She'd glimpsed the shadow side of their world and closing her eyes to the facts solved nothing. But today, she'd be everything her father wished because of the ball. This was Sidonie's triumph, her day of delight, and Miranda refused to spoil it.

Sadly, Olivia caught sight of Miranda on Sidonie's bed. *"That's what you're wearing tonight?"*

Miranda's party gown was a confection of soft cream net over peacock silk. "Yes," she said, wincing when it came out more apologetically than she liked.

Olivia's eyes went round. "Why didn't mine turn out like that?" Making a disgusted noise, she stormed from the room.

"Goodness." Sidonie shifted from the dressing table mirror to face Miranda. "One of us needs to go with her the next time she orders a gown."

Miranda sighed. "I'm sure everything will be fine by the time we get to Uncle's place."

"I do hope so. Public brawls are quite out of fashion this season."

The party was to be at the palatial home of their maternal uncle, the Earl of Havelock. Miranda's mother had been his youngest sister, and Sidonie was his favorite niece. Accordingly, the earl had invited half the world to dine, dance, and celebrate the engagement of Sidonie to Dr. Wilcox.

Deftly, Sidonie settled a tiara in her white-blonde locks. "Since I now have the jewelry right, what do you think?" She rose from the dressing table and made a curtsy.

Miranda caught her breath. "You're a vision."

Her sister's gown was made from layers of cream and white satin. The overskirt looped to her bustle, each fold edged in cloud-like layers of the finest Gallic lace. Tiny crystals were sown to every inch of the fabric, making Sidonie glitter like a star when she moved. Truly, she was the beauty of Londria. And yet, tears shimmered in her eyes.

Miranda pushed the litter of gloves aside, patting the bed beside her. "What's wrong?"

Sidonie sat. "It's going to be harder than I realized to leave this house."

"You have a good man with a good heart," Miranda said, taking her sister's hand. "You love each other so completely."

Sidonie swallowed hard. "I know."

"Besides which," Miranda continued, "I suspect Richard would like an actual wife out of this bargain, which means you can't stay here. You must be prepared to manage his house and play hostess at his dinner parties."

Sidonie laughed. "It will fall to you to help Father entertain once I'm gone. Olivia is not a viable candidate."

"Shall I invite a fortune teller?" Miranda asked with a mocking smile.

Sidonie rolled her eyes. "Heavens no, don't make my mistake. Papa still hasn't found out about Madam Alma."

Miranda rested her head against her sister's shoulder. Sidonie wrapped her arm around her younger sibling. They'd sat like this, the eldest and the youngest sisters together, ever since their mother's first illness years ago. Sidonie had been like another parent from the time Miranda had first learned her letters.

"I'm going to miss you," Miranda said. "Just so you know."

"It's only a marriage, and it won't happen for months."

"I'll miss having you here," Miranda said, "and being able to see you every day. I won't be aware of everything you do and vice versa. Not like I do now."

"You still have Gideon and Olivia," Sidonie pointed out, "though I admit they'll be a poor substitute."

They both chuckled as curses erupted from Olivia's bedroom. Their laughter felt good, but Miranda realized how sad she truly was.

"I should finish getting ready. May I borrow the cream gloves?" she asked.

"Of course." Sidonie hugged her close. "Promise me you'll enjoy yourself tonight."

"I will."

And yet, as Miranda left her sister's room, tears filled her eyes. It was ridiculous, but it felt as if her childhood was finally ending. Sidonie would only be the first of her siblings to go.

Miranda closed the door to her room, then glanced at the clock. She still had time. Crouching carefully so as not to wrinkle her dress, she lifted the corner of the carpet and pried the floorboards up where she'd concealed both the fortune-teller's cards and the book Mrs. Randall had brought her. Her fingers brushed the sandalwood box where she kept the cards, feeling a slight shiver course down her spine. Her imagination, surely, for the cards were just ink and paper. Still, she left them alone and picked up the book instead.

When Madam Alma had been hidden in the house, she'd read the girls' fortunes. She had predicted Olivia would grow rich—unsurprising given her sister's intellect. Miranda had received the scorpion card, along with Madam Alma's speech about its meaning. *The scorpion was small and insignificant, so Orion did not guard himself against its sting.*

But when it had come to Sidonie's fortune, Madam Alma, with expert sleight of hand, had changed one card for another. The second card had promised Sidonie true love and a sapphire ring, but the card before had been quite different.

Miranda had put Madam Alma's revision from her mind, but now she thumbed through the book in search of the original fortune. When she found it, she read the page twice.

THE COILED SERPENT is the resting arrow, conserving its energy before it strikes. It sheds its skin in transformation, but which form it takes next depends on the deepest truth of the heart.

While in its purest expression, the serpent represents wisdom and swift justice, but it can also depict extreme retribution. Beware this card, for the subject of the reading may be the victim or the instrument of vengeance. If the latter, the serpent brings temptation to indulge our darkest dreams.

The words of the serpent are transform, transcend, and terrorize.

MIRANDA CLOSED the book and returned it to its hiding place. She quickly slid the floorboards back into place, feeling as if she were imprisoning something wild and dangerous. There was no mystery why the fortune teller had chosen a different card—one that promised the marriage Sidonie wanted so much. The serpent card had to be wrong.

So why was Miranda questioning the outcome? Did she fear losing her siblings so much that she couldn't wish them well? Was she that selfish?

Tonight wasn't about her misgivings, she scolded herself. This was the time to celebrate love.

Miranda gathered her cloak and her borrowed gloves, then went downstairs to wait with her father and Gideon. Both were exquisite in their evening finery, watch chains gleaming against the silk of their waistcoats. Gideon nodded to her with a small smile, reading her mood. The dark circles under his eyes spoke of too much brandy and too little rest, but he was there as she was, putting on a good face.

"You look lovely," he said to her. "As always, of course. I would expect nothing less."

Miranda gave him a wry smile. "It's a great responsibility, but I can bear it."

Olivia descended a moment later. She'd made the right choice in her outfit at last, opting for the green dress Sidonie had suggested. The simple lines flattered, and the color gave a glow to her creamy skin as if her natural brilliance had found expression in the physical world.

Fletcher stepped forward, giving his middle daughter a kiss on the forehead. "You look like a queen."

Mollified at last, Olivia took her place at the foot of the stairs, her mood far more buoyant than it had been an hour ago. Miranda moved to stand beside her, companionably bumping shoulders as if they were still little girls.

Just as the carriages pulled up front, Sidonie floated down the stairs like a vision from a long-ago painting. Her glittering dress seemed to shine with a light of its own. She was rosy with happiness, her eyes bright and cheeks pink with anticipation for the night ahead.

"Wilcox is one fortunate man," Gideon said, taking her hand.

Although he was dark-haired and Sidonie fair, their profiles were alike—and so were their buoyant smiles. As Sidonie took Gideon's arm, his gloom seemed to fall away like melting frost beneath the sun of her pleasure. He escorted her out the door, taking the lead.

The twins, as well as Sidonie's maid, occupied the smaller of the two carriages. The rest of them took the other. As Miranda mounted the vehicle's steps, she glanced up to see the stars sparkling above.

Orion shone above, his bow glittering in the night.

CHAPTER 9

"I hate traffic," Olivia muttered, leaning her head out the carriage window.

"A crush is a mark of social success," Miranda replied. "This one is everything a couple wishing to rise in Society's ranks could desire."

They'd been inching forward at a snail's pace for the last half hour as each vehicle let down its passengers and pulled away from the Earl of Havelock's impressive front door. His home occupied one side of an elegant square in the west end of the city. The house itself had been built no more than a century ago, the style and elegant proportions straight from an architect's manual. Tall, fluted columns framed the entryway, supporting a triangular pediment carved with his coat of arms. The Fletchers mounted the steps together, the doors opening wide to admit the guests of honor. It was a reminder of how much Norton Fletcher had risen in the world, considering he had begun life as no more than a hardworking airman.

Inside, the throng was no less daunting. The girls hurried to the retiring rooms to leave their cloaks and put on their dancing shoes. An adjoining room had been set up with dressing tables and mirrors. Sidonie's maid, Wilson, pulled out her hairpins and brushes to ensure each Fletcher sister was flawless before they entered the ballroom. As Wilson worked, a steady stream of other ladies came and went. Everyone fussed over Sidonie, exclaiming over her good fortune. After all, Dr. Wilcox was handsome, wealthy, successful, and charming, all of which added up to a glittering future. Sidonie had made a fine catch.

Eventually, they rejoined the men at the head of the grand staircase. The majordomo announced their arrival in stentorian tones, and Sidonie descended on her father's arm. General applause rose from the ballroom. Olivia and Miranda each took one of Gideon's arms and followed. Miranda was delighted to be part of the moment, but equally happy to give pride of place to her sister.

Their uncle waited at the bottom of the stairs to greet them as he always did, happiness mixing with the flush of an exceptionally good brandy.

"Lovely to see you, my dears," he said, kissing the cheeks of the girls and clapping Gideon's shoulder. He was a tall, broad-shouldered man with fierce gray whiskers and a balding pate. "The countess and our brood are all in Hibernia this time of year. I'm grateful to have young folk about."

"How are the farms getting on?" Fletcher asked.

The earl waved a hand toward the party, letting the opulence speak for itself. "I have to thank you for encouraging me to buy the western properties. The investment has paid off handsomely."

Miranda had never been to the walled farms outside the city, but knew the earl had many tracts of agricultural land, as well as several Fletcher airships to patrol their borders. In addition, he kept representatives of the Conclave on retainer to keep his properties safe.

"I'm glad the deal worked out," Fletcher said. "We should sit and talk about a few other places that have caught my eye."

"You will have my full attention over a bottle of excellent

port." The earl grinned, which made his mustache bristle fiercely. Miranda recalled being slightly afraid of it as a child.

Fletcher laughed. "Ply me with your port, my lord, and I will be glad to share my recommendations."

With that, they entered the ballroom. Chandeliers glittered above, casting a glow over the company. An orchestra played on the balcony, and couples already danced. Once the family scattered, Miranda circled the floor in search of people she knew.

Unfortunately, the first person she saw was Councilor Ormond standing with a clutch of other blue-robed members of the Senior Council. Miranda silently cursed. While she hadn't actually seen him at Hellion House, he was easy to recognize. His likeness had been in the newspaper more than once, and that heavy-jawed face wasn't easy to forget. Of course, her uncle would have been obliged to invite representatives from the Citadel—nothing of consequence happened in the city without the Conclave's presence. Miranda felt the same superstitious shiver as when she touched Madam Alma's tarot cards. She glanced nervously at Ormond, then turned to walk the other way. She wasn't fast enough.

"Miss Miranda Fletcher," Ormond called, sailing toward her in a billow of robes. "I've been hoping to make the acquaintance of the younger members of your family."

Miranda made a low curtsy. "I am honored by your interest, sir."

"You have pretty manners, which does your father credit. Or was it your mother's doing? She was the connection to the earldom, was she not?"

"Yes, sir," Miranda said. Of course, Ormond already knew the answer to his question. For some reason, though, he wanted a conversation.

Ormond took her hand in his, his fleshy palm engulfing her fingers. "What do you think of the party, my dear?"

The shiver she'd felt before intensified, and she withdrew her hand as gracefully as she could. Was it the Conclave's magic or simply her own revulsion? "It's a fine party, sir. We are all grateful for it."

His smile was fatherly. "Happiness and prosperity should inspire gratitude. So should safety."

"We are grateful that the Citadel guards the city," she replied automatically. The words had been drilled into her from childhood.

He touched her cheek lightly. "The order we bring allows for nights like this, for your beautiful dresses, and for your soft beds. There is a reason we exist, Miss Miranda."

Ormond's tone said he'd delivered his message. Miranda sank into another curtsy, keeping her eyes on the floor as he moved away, his steps slow and stately.

Sudden tension made it difficult for Miranda to rise, as if her back and knees had locked in place. What had the conversation meant? Was it a warning? Had he somehow known she'd been at Mrs. Randall's?

There is a reason for everything, Miss Miranda.

What was she supposed to think? All she knew for certain was he'd unsettled her.

Miranda finally rose and flicked open her fan, cooling her face. She needed a moment to recover, but the ballroom wasn't the place. With hurried steps, she returned to the retiring room, hoping for a moment of quiet.

Happily, the room was empty even of the maids, who had been run off their feet earlier. Miranda sat at a mirror and adjusted a hairpin, letting her thoughts quiet.

She was being ridiculous. Certainly, Ormond was imposing, but she was jumping at shadows. She would return to the dancing and have a brilliant evening. After all, that was why she had come.

As she finished adjusting her hair, she heard voices in the

adjoining cloakroom. Miranda froze, realizing that one woman was crying.

"I don't know what happened," said a voice Miranda recognized. It was Elizabeth Morton, Kitty I-swoon-for-Gideon Morton's older sister. "We had an understanding. We were to be married next year, if everything went well. And now, he's suddenly gone."

Was she talking about Simeon Blanchard, Viscount Cornwell's son? Miranda's ears grew hot with embarrassment. Eavesdropping was hardly good behavior, but her curiosity was on full alert.

"I learned from his family he's become an acolyte at the Citadel. No warning—not even a mention of it before now. One day, he was on the dance floor. The next, I have no fiancé."

Miranda angled the mirror, so its reflection captured the doorway to the cloakroom. Now she could see a scrap of a rose-colored gown, but the speakers themselves were hidden. Miranda swiveled the mirror again, but the result was no better.

"That's horrible," another voice answered. It was Isobel Poole's, one of Miranda's friends from school. "Sadly, it's not the first time I've heard about something like this. Do you recall John Bartman?"

"I do," Elizabeth said.

"One day, he simply vanished never to be heard from again. No one could ever explain it. Not really."

The conversation fell silent, and Miranda heard the sound of sniffling. She rose from the dressing table as quietly as she could. Elizabeth was in good hands with Isobel, and the best Miranda could do was leave quietly to spare the girl any embarrassment. No one wanted to be caught weeping at someone else's engagement party. As Miranda left, she took one last glance toward the cloakroom, but the women were in shadows.

The conversation reminded Miranda of the meeting with Mrs.

Randall. She'd talked about disappearances as well. *People—especially young ones with money to spend—sometimes leave their homes without warning. Many fly to another city in search of novelty. Others unexpectedly join the Conclave, though I cannot fathom why.* Neither, apparently, could Simeon Blanchard's fiancée, and who could blame her?

Miranda had met John Bartman, and she remembered his disappearance. He had been part of the university set—rich, admired, heir to a title, and definitely not the type to hare off without warning. He'd had life by the tail and no reason to change a thing. When Miranda got back to the ballroom, she found Olivia, who had been dancing and was now delicately sipping lemonade to cool down.

"Livvy," Miranda said, leaning close so as not to be overheard. "You knew John Bartman, didn't you?"

"Yes. We attended classes together one term." Of course, Olivia hadn't settled for a ladies' college, but had insisted on the best possible schools.

"Do you know what happened to him?"

Olivia shook her head. "No. The word was academic pressure became too great for him, but I never believed he truly cared about such things."

"Don't you think that's odd?"

Annoyance flickered across Olivia's face. "Of course, but this is hardly the time to discuss it."

"Perhaps not, but..."

Olivia set her lemonade glass down on a passing servant's tray. "If you'll excuse me, I must say hello to Mrs. Peacock."

Then her sister was gone, leaving Miranda to fume. She couldn't be the only person to notice a pattern, but Olivia was right. This wasn't the right moment to discuss another family's grief.

But it never was. Manners prevented open discussion. Or was it fear? Would asking questions make the city crumble, depriving Society of their comfortable lives? Or as Ormond had put it—

beautiful dresses and soft beds? Everything happened for a reason.

Was she thinking like a coward?

The orchestra stopped, the sudden silence forcing Miranda out of her reverie. The Earl of Havelock took the floor, Fletcher at his side. Another man joined them—Dr. Charles Wilcox, Richard's father. The elder Wilcox ran the city's hospital, so it was natural that his son had made a career in medicine.

Fletcher began speaking, using the same carrying tone he used to order a dirigible's crew. "First, I would like to thank Havelock, our gracious host, for bringing us together tonight. As you all know, we're here for an extraordinarily happy occasion. I'm pleased to announce the engagement of my daughter, Sidonie Alicia Fletcher, to Dr. Richard William Wilcox."

There were cheers, raised glasses, and a general uproar of approval. Brief speeches followed from the father of the groom, the earl, then finally Richard. Miranda listened to her future brother-in-law with extra interest. If his encounter with the Conclave had left a mark in mind or body, he was careful not to let it show.

"I am so extremely pleased to have this wonderful woman at my side for the rest of my life," he said, taking Sidonie's hand and drawing her to his side. "My dear, I would like to take this occasion to give you a token of my promise and my love."

He drew a ring from the pocket of his waistcoat, then slid it onto her slender finger. Miranda caught a gleam of sapphires— the ring Madam Alma had promised. Her sister's face was suffused with happiness.

"And now," Wilcox said to Sidonie, a smile flashing across his dark face, "I would very much like to ask you to dance."

The orchestra started again. The couple began to circle the dance floor, their movements almost weightless. Miranda's heart ached with love for them both. Richard was a good dancer, but Sidonie melded with the music in a way few people could. Perhaps it was because she had been born to a family of airmen, but she positively flew around the marble tiles of the ballroom.

"Would you like to join them?"

The question had come from Miranda's right. She turned to see an unfamiliar young man. He was very handsome, with a lean jaw and high, prominent cheekbones. His jet-black hair made a startling contrast to his pale skin. Few men caught Miranda's attention, but this one did.

"I'm sorry to decline, but we haven't been introduced," she said, but tempered her refusal with a smile.

"Then I must remedy the situation. My name is William Kitteridge."

The Kitteridge family was tied by blood to the Grand Duke of Londria. She would have few chances to meet someone of his rank, much less dance with him. Still, she was slightly annoyed. "Does that mean I should waive all the social rules because you have an illustrious last name?"

"Forgive my presumption," he replied. "I'm sure if we search for a moment, I could find a dowager who could vouch for my character."

"And by then, the dance will be over, I suppose." Miranda sighed from behind her fan. "Very well, Mr. Kitteridge, I revoke my earlier words. Show me if your good breeding extends to a creditable waltz."

Apparently, it did. He led her smoothly between the other couples, executing the turns in a way that left her pleasantly breathless. "You have the advantage of me," he said after a moment. "I believe you are one of the Fletcher family, yes?"

"Miss Miranda Fletcher."

"Ah, I've heard of you." His eyes crinkled with a smile. "You're the one who flies airships."

"Indeed, I'm the family eccentric," she said lightly. "I read books, fly ships, and fire guns."

"Ah," he said cautiously. "You sound unimpressed with my conversational gambit."

She laughed. "It's the one thing I hear about myself—I'm the pampered girl who can pilot an airship."

"It's not a bad reputation to have. You could be remembered for atrocities at the piano."

"Society does enjoy labeling its members. It saves the work of actually getting to know a person."

"Touché." His smile widened. "I will work harder for your acquaintance, Miss Fletcher."

"So you should. I'm worth the time."

The conversation dwindled as they spun for a dozen beats of the song. She was conscious of his touch, of the coiled energy of his frame. His dark gray eyes spoke of a clever but restless spirit.

He tried again. "You mentioned firing guns. I take it you have an interest in firearms?"

"I do. I'm actually interested in aether weapons." She said it to throw him off his stride—to be one degree more outrageous—but he surprised her.

"It just so happens I know something of the technology," he said. "I've been studying at the University of Stonegate. They have been eager to master the possibilities of aether beyond simple flight."

Now she was intrigued. "You went away to study in another city? What was it like?"

"Stonegate is similar to Londria. I've traveled to the Continent, and there one can see some unique things."

Travel was for the truly rich. Even as the daughter of Norton Fletcher, she hadn't gone far. For the first time, she felt the gap in social rank between herself and this young man, and she didn't enjoy it. "So how does one find out about aether technology without traveling north? I've engaged a maker to produce a weapon for me, but she's run into difficulties."

She'd made the arrangements with Mrs. Randall, before

they'd left the Mercury. Janey had sent two separate messages seeking clarification of Miranda's design, but progress had been slow.

"I might have some helpful books. Perhaps you should visit me to peruse my volumes." The grin he gave her was enigmatic at best. Would she go for the library, but stay for seduction?

The dance was ending. Kitteridge lifted her hand and brushed a kiss to her gloved fingers. "Perhaps I can reserve a dance later?"

Miranda blushed, but then hated herself for it. "If you promise to tell me more about your studies."

"I can regale you with fascinating tales of polarity and resistance."

"I am breathless with anticipation."

"Good." His smile was lopsided, but truly genuine for once. "Allow me to bring you some refreshments."

Miranda watched Kitteridge disappear into the crowd, not quite sure what to make of him.

Just then, Sidonie appeared beside her in a rustle of glitter and lace. Tears shimmered in her eyes as she hugged Miranda tight. "What is it?" Miranda asked, afraid something was wrong.

"I'm so happy," Sidonie said. "If you ever find someone—or even something—who makes you feel this way, hold it tight."

"Of course."

"Promise me, my dear."

"I do."

CHAPTER 10

The ball ended just before dawn. Gideon had passed through a state of fatigue to a lightheaded buoyancy sometime after the midnight supper. He'd danced a set of polkas with Kitty Morton, and she'd turned out to be a far less objectionable partner than he had assumed. Maybe Miranda would get her hands on the family's telescope after all.

Eventually, they gathered in the house's massive entryway to take their leave. A steady stream of carriages paused at the curb, collecting the partygoers they'd delivered hours before. By the time the Fletchers were ready to go, only a few carriages remained.

Gideon stood by the door, hoping the fresh air would keep him awake. His sisters had enjoyed themselves, if he were any judge. Sidonie, of course, was delirious with joy. Olivia had galloped around the ballroom for hours on end, and she was now yawning her way into her cloak and gloves. It was Miranda who gave Gideon pause.

"You spent rather a long time in William Kitteridge's company," he observed, trying his best to sound casual. "It's bound to cause comment, so I hope the conversation was worth your trouble."

Miranda studied him from beneath her lashes. "He had something to say for himself."

Her defensive tone put Gideon on alert. It was hard to look at his sister like a suitor instead of a sibling. In his mind's eye, Miranda was still a young girl in braids. In truth, however, she was a dark-haired sylph with large dark eyes and creamy skin.

It was enough to rouse Gideon's protective streak to a fever pitch. "I don't know this Kitteridge myself, but the word on the street is he's a remorseless heartbreaker."

A cloud passed over Miranda's features, and he felt cruel. "Don't spoil my evening," she said. "And don't concern yourself. We share an interest in a few subject areas, that's all."

An apology was on the tip of Gideon's tongue, but he ran out of time to make it. Sidonie chose that moment to float into the marble entryway, her face wreathed in smiles.

"Thank you so, so much, Uncle," she said, kissing the earl's cheek. "You've been a most generous and perfect host."

Their uncle rumbled and huffed with pleasure. "I'm proud of you, my darling," he said to Sidonie. "You will be a most beautiful bride."

As they made their goodbyes, the Kitteridges decided to leave as well. On their way out, they paused to pay their respects to the earl. William was deferential, taking his cue from his grandfather and saying all the right things. He tipped his hat to the Fletchers, then gave a slight bow to Miranda as they took their leave.

Gideon watched the exchange carefully, but there was nothing to justify his concern until Sidonie gave Miranda a knowing smile. He'd have to say something to his twin about safeguarding Miranda's affections against a spoiled lordling.

Especially this one. Baron Kitteridge was William's grandfather, and he had adopted the boy on the death of his daughter and her husband. Naturally, the old man had given the orphaned child the best of everything. And yet, Gideon wasn't sure he'd call William lucky. The family had money and connections, but there was something unwholesome about their great crumbling house overlooking the heath. It reminded Gideon of a mausoleum.

He dropped that train of thought as they began loading the carriages. Miranda, Olivia, and Norton Fletcher made their getaway in good order, but Sidonie dawdled with an endless stream of well-wishers. It was a good ten minutes later when Gideon handed her into their carriage and the vehicle finally left the drive. Sidonie's maid, Wilson, rode up top with the groom, who was driving. Gideon suspected a romance, because nothing else would explain why the woman refused a warm seat inside.

The temperature had dropped, a layer of cloud moving in overnight. Gideon peered out the carriage window to see the first pale streaks in the east, then dropped the curtain with a jaw-cracking yawn. He was used to staying out late, but he'd been pushing his limits over the last few weeks. The carriage rocked gently. Sidonie was silent, lost in her own thoughts. Gideon drowsed, then slid into sleep.

He wasn't sure how much time had passed when he was jolted back to consciousness. He peered out the window, squinting to bring the view into focus. Their route took them through the Grove of Angels Cemetery, and the winding path played hide and seek through layers of fog. The carriage lanterns made exotic blooms in the damp air, barely lighting more than a few yards ahead. He could see snow falling a flake at a time, melting as soon as it touched the gravestones. Perhaps it was his fatigue talking, but he suddenly wished they had guards.

"You're nervous," Sidonie said.

"I'm wondering how far we are from home."

"A half hour at least."

Gideon swore. "We can go faster than this."

Sidonie studied him. "You know, Richard was badly shaken by his experience at Hellion House. He told me about the incident, or at least what he decided I should hear."

"And?"

"I know you were there, and that you're carrying a pistol right now."

"That's not new."

"Even for you, it's an unusual accessory for a formal ball. Not even your exalted tailor can quite hide the bulge."

Gideon dropped the curtain, reclining against the squabs of the carriage. "I confess, the incident left me nervous."

"There's no shame in that," Sidonie said. "Without this party, I'm certain Richard would have dwelled on the whole episode far too much."

She didn't see the torn body, Gideon thought. If she had, she would have realized how completely a sight like that colored one's mind.

One of the horses gave a startled neigh. The carriage lurched to a halt, throwing Gideon forward. Then he heard Wilson screaming—a high, piteous sound.

Gideon recovered his balance, but not fast enough. The door on Sidonie's side of the carriage flung open, and a clawed hand swept in. She'd barely let out a shriek before she was dragged into the darkness. Gideon flung open his door and leaped out, pistol in hand.

His boots had just hit the dirt when the horses bolted, dragging the rattling carriage after them. Terror twisted in Gideon's chest. He was stranded and alone...but not alone.

"Sidonie?"

He made a slow turn, searching the swirling fog. A flash of motion caught his eye—the white gleam of Sidonie's gown. Fear turned to fury. He bolted toward it, banging his shin on a tombstone.

Stone angels leered from the darkness, wings looming above him as he ran. Soon, he made out two figures, each dragging his sister by an arm. She was stumbling and falling, her long skirts tangling her feet. He dared not shoot—visibility was bad, and the odds of hitting his sister were high. Instead, Gideon pressed on, deafened by his own gasping breath, until he was almost upon them. He lunged, his fingers brushing Sidonie's cloak. Another step, and his fingers could grasp it.

Pain shot through the back of his head.

He fell, rolling and fumbling for his pistol. As his hand closed over the grip, a weight landed on him, knocking the breath from his lungs. The leering face of an Unseen filled his vision, its ragged teeth snapping at his eyes. Limp brown hair straggled from its skull, its skin sagging from fleshless bones. With a roar of revulsion, he shoved it away, but it clung like a monkey, its arms and legs wrapping around Gideon's frame. Beyond mercy, Gideon pressed the gun to the underside of its chin and fired. The creature exploded backward in a shower of gore.

Gideon scrambled to his feet with a shudder, firing again into the headless body just in case. *Unseen.* His gorge rose, memories crowding in. Black. Tupper. The cold despair of knowing the Unseen were beyond the wall, and there was nothing anyone could do about it.

And now the abominations were inside.

He saw Sidonie a dozen yards ahead. Since he now knew what they faced, he had a duty. He raised his pistol, intending to spare her from the horrors to come. His hand shook, the grip slippery against his palm. Gideon made a sound between a cry and a groan of despair. His finger refused to pull the trigger. Not on his twin.

A male voice shouted. The words were lost in the fog, but the grass rustled as a dozen Unseen erupted from the graveyard, loping toward the figures carrying Sidonie away.

Fright cleared Gideon's mind. Steadying his breath, he took aim. Just as he pulled the trigger, the figure at Sidonie's left turned and looked back.

Human.

The shot went wide.

Something clubbed him from behind. Again.

~

"Miranda. Miranda, wake up."

Olivia's insistent voice floated through the fog of sleep. Miranda cracked open her eyes as her sister shook her. She grunted in protest, batting Olivia away as her eyes focused on the fuzzy gray light invading her bedroom. The frigid air beyond the nest of her blankets said the fire hadn't been lit.

"What time is it?" she protested. "And why are you dressed?"

"It's just gone seven," her sister replied. "The house is in an uproar."

"What's wrong?"

"Sidonie and Gideon never came home," Olivia said, her voice grave.

Miranda sat up, heedless of the chill. "What?"

"Papa sat up waiting for them, and he eventually began to worry. He sent one of the footmen over to Dr. Wilcox's house to see if they'd gone there for some reason, but they hadn't. Now Dr. Wilcox and Papa have gone searching, along with most of the servants."

Miranda opened her mouth, but nothing came out.

"What woke me up," Olivia continued, "was a commotion outside my bedroom window. Jackson found the horses wandering just south of the Grove of Angels Cemetery. It seems one of the horses lost its shoe, but is otherwise unharmed."

"What about the groom? And Wilson?"

"There's been no sign of them."

Miranda pushed out from under the covers. "Help me get dressed." She didn't have the patience to wait for her own maid.

Olivia's hands were cold as she did the buttons up the back of Miranda's dress. With her hair in a simple braid, Miranda followed her sister downstairs to the kitchen, where the remaining servants were preparing breakfast. The spacious room felt empty with only half the staff present.

"Any news, Mrs. Vern?" Miranda asked the cook, who was kneading dough.

"No, my dears," the cook answered, pausing long enough to give them a tight smile.

The woman had been with the household since before Miranda had been born. She had the same worn expression as when Miranda's mother was ill.

Dusting the flour off her hands, the cook reached for an enormous pewter teapot. She poured two cups, adding a generous amount of milk and sugar, then handed one to each young woman. "Drink this to warm up. You'll need your strength today, I fear."

Mechanically, Miranda took a swallow of the milky tea. It went down thick and sweet, chasing away the last cobwebs clinging to her thoughts.

The rattle of carriage wheels outside sent them scurrying up the steps from the kitchen. The housemaid opened the front door, and Dr. Wilcox burst in. One of the footmen and her father carried something up the front steps. Not something. *Someone.*

Gideon. Blood soaked his shirt.

Beside Miranda, Olivia moaned in dismay.

Miranda's mouth went dry. The scene was eerily similar to the one at Hellion House. Miranda's vision began to go black at the edges.

Dr. Wilcox spoke in a firm, clear voice. "We need to get him to bed."

Miranda returned to life. "Take him upstairs. Someone clear a path."

Olivia sprang into action, running ahead to open doors.

"Where's Mrs. Trencher?" Miranda demanded, frantically looking for the housekeeper. She spotted the woman standing by the door to the salon. "Bring all the medical supplies we have."

The older woman bobbed her head. "At once, Miss Miranda."

Wilcox and the groom carried Gideon upstairs. Fletcher sat heavily on the bench by the door. "Thank you for taking over," he said wearily. "We have not found *her*. Not yet."

Sidonie was still missing. Miranda felt faint again, but resolutely pushed the sensation aside. "Are there any signs of the others?"

"No." The lines in Fletcher's face seemed deeper than before.

Miranda sat beside him, taking his hand. "You need to rest."

"I need my daughter." Fletcher put his head in his hands. "What happened? They say there was no damage to the vehicle, so where did everyone go?"

A housemaid arrived with a cup of tea, and Miranda pressed it into her father's hands. "Drink," she said. "I insist."

Fletcher's hands were shaking, so she cupped hers around them as he drank. He fixed her with a level gaze. "Gideon must wake up. He's the only witness we have."

Miranda straightened, wondering if her brother would indeed wake up at all. Her breath hitched, fear making it hard to draw breath.

"Go," her father said. "I'll be all right. As soon as I've rested a moment, I'm going back out to look for…for your sister."

Miranda noticed the hesitation. He hadn't said Sidonie's name, as if he could not bear the feel of it on his tongue. She put her arms around him, hugging him close. "Everything will be all right. It has to be."

Her father said nothing, but he held her as if he would never let her go.

Not long after, she went upstairs, taking the steps almost reluctantly. When she reached Gideon's room, Dr. Wilcox was standing by the bed, examining her brother's scalp. He'd washed the blood away, and now she could see bruises and swelling on one side of Gideon's forehead. Wilcox glanced her way as she entered.

"He suffered a head injury," he said. "No bites or scratches."

Miranda released her breath. "What does that tell us?"

"I'm just a doctor," Wilcox said, his voice rough with grief. "All I can say is that his injuries appear to have been caused by ordinary violence."

"Will he be all right?" Miranda asked.

"Yes, I believe so," Wilcox said. "It's difficult to tell with head injuries, but I've done what I can for now. All we can do is wait."

Miranda circled the bed to get a better look at her brother. He seemed exhausted, even now. "Have the authorities been notified?"

Wilcox nodded. "Inspector Palmer has been summoned."

There was an unhealthy sheen to the doctor's skin. A sign of nerves, Miranda guessed, or shock.

"Then why don't you return to the search?" she suggested. "Olivia and I can watch Gideon."

"Thank you." The doctor closed his eyes, clearly torn between the duty to his patient and the one to his love.

Miranda's heart hurt for him. "Go."

Wilcox left after giving instructions to summon him if there was any change. Olivia came in and sat in a chair beside Miranda's, her hands twitching nervously in her lap. Gideon breathed quietly, but everything else in the room was still.

"I don't know if I can sit here all day," Olivia said. "This is awful."

Miranda didn't reply.

"We could play cards," Olivia said.

Miranda rose and looked out the window. The snow had turned to rain.

Cards.

The scorpion. The coiled serpent.

The subject of the reading may be the victim or the instrument of vengeance.

"I'm not in the mood for cards."

CHAPTER 11

Gideon opened his eyes to a brilliant flare. The light seared his brain from the back of his eyeballs to the marrow of his skull. He blinked, squeezing his eyes shut. Warm tears tracked over his cheeks, and a red haze danced across the backs of his lids.

Cautiously, he cracked his eyes open again. The room was dark except for one explosion of light. Slowly, he understood it was a flame. Dazzled, he averted his gaze, then recognized his bedroom. How had he come to be here? His memory was nothing but a murky haze.

Thunk. The room was dark except for the glow of coals in the grate. A few seconds later, he heard a click and whir. Another explosion of light flared—only to vanish with another *thunk.* Curious now, Gideon slid his gaze toward the disturbance. After a fuzzy moment, the figure seated at the end of his bed resolved into Inspector Palmer.

As bedside companions went, Palmer wouldn't have been Gideon's choice. The man was unshaven and slouched in the chair with his chin to his chest. His frock coat was unbuttoned to show a striped waistcoat of the kind favored by the absinthe-drinking radicals. Either Palmer had a rebellious streak, or the fashion sense of a turnip.

More to the point, why was the man here?

Gideon was distracted by the flame again. Palmer held a complicated lighter in one hand. When he spun a wheel with his thumb, a tiny brass dragon reared up and breathed flame, until the wheel was released and the contraption snapped shut again. That was the sound he'd heard. Gideon's mind snagged on the fact the dragons didn't actually breathe flame, but there was something more important…something he should recall…but he couldn't. His head pounded with every beat of his pulse.

Sighing, he sank back into his pillow. The motion caught Palmer's attention, and he slid the lighter into his coat pocket. He eyed Gideon with a furrowed brow. "How are you feeling?"

It was a good question. Was this a hangover? Had Gideon done something requiring Palmer's presence? His mouth tasted as if it were filled with glue.

"I'm not sure." It came out in a croak.

Then he remembered. He'd been at Sidonie's engagement ball.

It was like the corner piece of a puzzle. Having seized that much, more came back. He recalled leaving the party and getting into the carriage, the conversation with Sidonie about Wilcox. After that, his knees had hit the grass. It had been snowing. Even before the last of the images filled in, a torrent of guilt crashed through him. *I failed. I didn't save her.*

He reached up, fumbling at the bandage wrapped around his head. "What happened?"

"We found you in the cemetery."

Gideon let his arm drop as memory swirled. Why the cemetery? Of course—they had to cross it to come home. There had been snow and darkness and…

Palmer leaned forward, his elbows on his knees. "You are the only witness besides the horses, but they're not talking."

Horses. They'd bolted, taking the carriage and leaving Gideon alone. The recollection came with a rush of blinding terror. "You found the horses?"

"And the carriage. It wasn't damaged."

It was like Gideon's memory had been thinly sliced and was being served back to him, one shaving at a time. "What else?"

"The maid and the driver were found in the cemetery." Palmer's voice was flat, free of all emotion. "There was enough clothing left to identify the remains."

A rush of images crowded in. Black. Tupper. The mop-up from the missions Gideon had flown, when he'd gone into the forest to rescue travelers who had gone astray. Nothing left but broken bones, the marrows licked clean. His mind circled around and around, purposefully avoiding the One Thing he couldn't bear to hear. *What happened to my sister?*

"Now you know what we know." Palmer's voice was gentler than before. "It's time you helped us. Who attacked the carriage?"

Gideon's memory ebbed away like the tide, but he grabbed one fact before it disappeared. "I killed one of them."

"We found your pistol. It had been fired."

"The body?"

Palmer shook his head. "If there was a body, someone removed it."

"If?"

"There's no evidence. Who do you think you killed?" A hard note in Palmer's voice reminded Gideon who he was talking to.

"Unseen. It was an ambush. At least a dozen hid behind the headstones."

"I didn't know they hunted in a coordinated way," Palmer said, the words carefully neutral.

"We don't really know how they hunt," Gideon said. "No one has survived to tell us."

He'd stood with his gun raised and his hands shaking. He remembered the chill of sweat trickling down his temples. His chest had ached, his breath ragged with anger and remorse for what he had to do. What he'd done for Black. He could still feel the slippery grip of the pistol as he tried to squeeze the trigger, but, like a coward, he couldn't kill her, his sister, his twin. She'd been at his side before he'd even been born.

Grief tore the last veils from his mind. "It wasn't just Unseen. Men dragged Sidonie away."

Palmer stood suddenly, as if he'd been startled. "Tell me more."

Gideon struggled to sit up. Palmer helped, arranging the pillows with the efficiency of a nurse.

"They were human," Gideon said. "The ones who took my sister."

Palmer's eyes narrowed. "Humans and Unseen working together?"

Gideon was aware how strange that sounded. "The humans were in charge."

"Describe them."

"It was dark." Gideon tried to conjure the scene, but they'd been in the shadows.

"What were they wearing?" Palmer asked, producing a notebook from his pocket and flipping it open to write.

"Their clothes were dark."

"There were two humans in dark clothing," Palmer repeated. "Is that all?"

"I'm sorry."

Palmer scratched his jaw, the stubble rasping. "Did they have robes?"

Were they with the Conclave? Gideon wanted that. It would have been satisfying to blame someone he distrusted already, but he couldn't. "No. No robes."

"Top hats? Any hats?"

"They were low crowned." That meant they weren't from the top echelons of the city.

"Frock coats or worker's smock?"

"I'm not sure. Caped coats, I think."

Palmer continued writing.

Gideon swallowed hard, forcing himself to face the worst. "I take it you've found no sign of my sister."

Palmer's pencil stopped, but he didn't look up. "No, we haven't."

Guilt pulsed in Gideon's blood. *I should have saved her. I should have been faster.* "I need to help."

"You are helping." Palmer fixed him with a hard look. "But you're hurt. You'll only slow us down if you join the search."

"I can't stay here," Gideon said. He sat up, swinging his legs over the edge of the bed. A crippling dizziness made him clutch the edge of the mattress. He ground his teeth, forcing himself not to sway.

"Give us today," Palmer said. "My lads are out combing every inch of the cemetery. I'll leave them at it as long as I can."

"What does that mean?" Gideon asked.

"When a young woman from a good family is snatched coming home from a ball, the public demands answers. Unfortunately, I'm not sure what my men will find, or what they'll be allowed to find, if you take my meaning."

Gideon did. Palmer had been at Hellion House when the Conclave arrived. "You weren't allowed to investigate Tupper's murder, were you?"

"Unfortunately, we did not have that pleasure," the inspector replied dryly. "In a similar vein, we took the remains of your servants to a police surgeon for examination, but the bodies disappeared. I've already told your father to start spreading a tale about highwaymen with a side serving of wolves. Better not to start talking about monsters who aren't supposed to be there. We don't want the Conclave paying your house a visit."

Gideon raised his head. "Where does that leave my sister?"

"I don't give up easily. I'll find an answer, even if it's not the one you want."

"While you're at it, get me two answers," Gideon said.

Palmer frowned. "Explain."

"I want my sister back. I also want to know why the monsters left me alive."

NURSING WAS NOT Olivia's typical role, but she performed it conscientiously until Gideon was well enough to leave the house. When she wasn't relieving her sister, Miranda journeyed back to the graveyard with Dr. Wilcox and the others. Although Palmer's constables had already searched there, the family combed through the gravesites again, hunting for the minutest clue. They found mud and frost but no sign of Sidonie. Eventually, a soaking rain obliterated every footprint.

On the third day, Miranda came home cold and miserable. After shedding her sodden cloak and boots, she climbed the stairs, heading to her bedroom to change her gown. The garment she wore was soaked to her knees, and her muddy petticoats clung to her stockings with every step.

As she went down the hall, she noticed the door to Sidonie's room was open. Lamplight spilled into the corridor. Miranda's heart leaped. She ran forward, hope a physical ache. Had her sister come home?

But when Miranda reached the room, she fell back in surprise. Olivia had every drawer and cupboard open. All of Sidonie's things were scattered across the floor and the white counterpane of her bed.

"What are you doing?" Miranda cried.

Olivia jerked her head up, her face creased with anger. "There has to be something in her belongings that will give us a clue."

Miranda was tongue-tied. She knew about the Unseen

because she'd been present at Tupper's death, but Gideon had kept the information secret from Olivia. At first, Miranda had disagreed—but after reflecting on Ormond's conversation at the ball, secrecy seemed prudent. The less Olivia knew, the safer she was, and Miranda wasn't about to jeopardize another family member.

Miranda chose her words carefully. "You don't think Sidonie was taken because of something she did, do you?"

Even as she said it, she saw Olivia's idea had merit. Gideon had told her what had happened in the Grove of Angels. Unseen were there, but so were human kidnappers. They had to be working together, but why? That notion terrified her more than anything else.

"Think about this logically," Olivia snapped. "Has there been a ransom? Was the coach robbed? No and no. Was this the work of an angry rebel mob striking back at those with money? No, Gideon was left alive. The villains took what they came for, and nothing more."

"What you're saying makes sense." Miranda drew near Olivia's side. The scent of Sidonie's perfume was so familiar it nearly made her weep. "Have you found anything?"

"Not yet." Olivia collapsed on the edge the bed. "I've been thinking about John Bartman as well. Where do young people disappear to? Another city? A ship? The Citadel?

Miranda pondered. "Gideon said none of the attackers wore robes."

"Who says kidnapping requires a robe?" Olivia snapped. "There are such things as disguises."

Her sister had a point, but why would the Conclave work with the Unseen? That made no sense at all. Miranda sat next to Olivia, stroking her hair.

Olivia's expression crumpled. "I don't understand what's happening."

"We'll find her," Miranda said, terribly afraid she was lying.

Tears tracked down Olivia's face. "I hate this. I hate that I can't solve it. It's an equation out of balance."

Miranda slipped her arms around her sister's shoulders and drew her close, tears hot on her cheeks.

CHAPTER 12

Inspector Palmer and his men found no trace of Sidonie. As each day passed, Allington House sank deeper into gloom, as if the bleak mood dimmed every color. Coffins representing the deceased servants—only a few souls aware they contained no bodies—were quietly buried. Shortly after that, the coach and horses were sold. No one could bear to look at the vehicle any longer.

Two days after the funeral, Miranda sat in the morning room, combing the newspaper for any possible clues. She wasn't sure what she hoped to find—she didn't read the detective novels Gideon devoured—but she hadn't given up searching. Olivia hovered at the window, staring in silent contemplation at the pedestrians and carriages passing by. It was almost as if she expected Sidonie to simply walk up the steps and ask about luncheon.

"I believe we have visitors," Olivia said dully.

"Who?"

Olivia didn't answer, and Miranda heard footfalls on the stairs. She rose just as Councilor Ormond entered. Heart in her mouth, Miranda gave a deep curtsy.

"Do I find you alone, Miss Miranda?" Ormond said.

Olivia turned from the window, startling him. She'd been so still Ormond had missed her. "I will see if Father is at home to visitors," she said, abruptly leaving the room.

"Please forgive my sister's manners," Miranda said. "She's still very upset."

"Of course." Ormond sat, not waiting for an invitation to make himself comfortable. He regarded Miranda as he had the night of the ball, as if sizing up a lamb for his dinner table.

"May I offer you refreshments?" Miranda asked, refusing to be rattled.

"Some port, I think."

"I will ask Jeffries to fetch some," Fletcher said as he entered the room. He tugged the bell pull to summon a servant, then offered the councilor a bow. "How gracious of you to visit."

"Not at all."

"Miranda, you may go."

"On the contrary." Ormond clasped his hands over his ample stomach, giving a beatific smile. "I come to console and guide the entire family. There is no need to send your lovely daughter away."

With an unhappy expression, Fletcher sank down beside Miranda on the divan. The ordeal of the last weeks had been hard on her father. He had succumbed to a chill after spending so much time in the rain and wind, and his breathing still sounded rough.

"This is a terrible time," Ormond said, his voice blandly sympathetic. "Your loss has been upsetting for the entire community."

He glanced around at the many sympathy bouquets crowding the room. Most were starting to drop their petals. "Perhaps it's time to look forward once more."

"What are you suggesting?" Fletcher asked.

Ormond stretched out his legs. "My job as a council member

is to ensure public harmony is maintained. Grief has its season, but no season lasts forever."

He was interrupted by the arrival of the butler, Jeffries, who began dispensing port. Ormond held his glass up to the light, admiring the ruby shade.

"Fletcher Industries must be seen to carry on as before," Ormond said, taking a delicate sip from the crystal glass. "Airships are vital to Londria's wellbeing, and the Citadel feels public confidence in your enterprise serves the community."

"I don't understand," Fletcher said.

"Your continued search for Miss Fletcher is upsetting to many. Mourning is expected, but the true business of life must go on."

"But we don't know for certain that Sidonie is lost to us," Miranda interjected. She was unable to say *dead*. Not yet.

"We have not given up hope," Fletcher added.

"Hope is essential to life," Ormond said agreeably. "But so is realism."

Fletcher bristled, his hands clenched in his lap so tightly his knuckles turned white. Normally, he would allow his temper to explode, but this was a Senior Councilor. An outburst could destroy what remained of the family.

Miranda jumped in. "Isn't there something the Citadel can do? Can't *you* find my sister?"

"My dear," Ormond said, for the first time sounding genuinely sorrowful, "I would if I could. Remember, I was at your uncle's ball. I saw how happy your sister was. Unfortunately, the power of the Conclave is not designed for such a task."

There was a ring of truth in his words. Reluctantly, Miranda believed him.

"Let me say this again," Ormond continued, his voice firm. "The longer the search continues, the more the public speculates about Miss Fletcher's fate. Nonsense fills their heads, wild rumors circulate, and that leads to unrest. For the sake of public peace, it's time to close this matter quietly."

Ormond finished his port before rising. Miranda and her father stood also. Fletcher trembled with anger, but said nothing.

The councilor cleared his throat. "Advise your son of what I have said. I know he is an independent young man, but the Citadel expects him to show respect."

Miranda stiffened. Ormond's guards had smashed the windows of Hellion House simply because Mrs. Randall had spoken up on behalf of Tupper's family. It would be foolish to disobey.

But he's asking us to abandon Sidonie.

They made stiff farewells, and Ormond left. Miranda crossed to the window to watch him go. A pair of Conclave guards stood outside the front door, and they fell into step like ducklings as the councilor crossed the street to his fine black carriage.

"Gideon is not going to accept those orders easily," Miranda commented to her father.

"He'll have to." Her father began to cough, and he downed his glass of port in a single swallow.

Miranda watched her father uneasily, worrying about his health. *If only we had certainty, he could rest.*

Even as she thought it, she knew that was a distant dream.

THE NEXT MORNING, Miranda received another letter from Mrs. Randall. She waited until she was alone in her bedroom to open it. It was on the same cream paper and written in the same violet ink the woman had used before. The note was brief.

MY DEAR MISS FLETCHER,

There is no need for me to embellish upon your grief. Let me say simply that my thoughts are with you.
With greatest respect,
G. R.

BELOW THE FLOURISH of initials was a postscript.

WHEN YOU ARE able to think of such things, Janey would like a word about your project. You know where we are.

THE LAST LINE was like opening a window to let in the spring breeze. After almost a week of constant frustration, Miranda needed a change of scenery. Even an hour away from the house would lift her spirits.

Still, venturing to Hellion House was riskier than meeting at the café. This wasn't a visit she should make lightly. In fact, it went against every scrap of advice given to respectable young ladies.

And, before the ball, Miranda would have hesitated out of concern for her safety and reputation. But she was commissioning a weapon, after all. Her family was grappling with matters of life and death. She was in a reckless mood.

Miranda found a thicker veil and a larger pistol. Then she asked the coachman to drive her to Dobson's bookshop and leave her there for an hour. Once the curricle was out of sight, Miranda made the quick walk to Maudlin Way.

Perhaps it was Miranda's determined frame of mind, but the occupants of the street let her pass without a murmur. When she knocked on the front door, Mrs. Randall quickly opened it herself, sparing her any encounters with servants or guests.

"I saw you from the window," she said, ushering Miranda inside. "I'm so glad you decided to come."

The woman's manner was gracious but matter of fact. As they stood in the entryway, a thump sounded from the floor above, followed by a guffaw of female laughter. Miranda froze with embarrassment, then chose to ignore the noise.

"Thank you for your letter," she said a little primly. "I came as soon as I read about Janey's project."

Mrs. Randall's eyes twinkled. "Of course. I'll take you to see her at once."

She led Miranda through the house to a surprisingly spacious back garden. There were apple trees and a scatter of late flowers. A path led to an outbuilding that might have once been a small carriage house. The door stood open, and the sound of someone pounding on metal filled the air.

With a dainty gesture, Mrs. Randall tugged on a small chain dangling from a brass box above the door. A shrill whistle and gust of steam emerged. The pounding stopped abruptly.

A moment later, Janey emerged into the sunlight, blinking behind her goggles. She pushed up the eyewear to reveal striking green eyes.

"Oh, hello, Miss Fletcher," she said cheerfully, wiping a smear of grease across her cheek. "I have something for you."

"I will leave you two to your discussion," Mrs. Randall said, retreating down the path to the house.

With a wave, Janey beckoned Miranda inside her workspace. It was a single room with workbenches on two sides. The walls were covered in wooden shelves that held jars of nails and tins of screws, bins of nuts and bolts, and endless containers of gears. Half-made projects sat everywhere. There was something squid-shaped that might have been a lamp, and a working dirigible the size of an orange. On the third surface sat a motionless ginger cat.

"He's flesh and blood," Janey said. "Don't pet him if you want to keep your hand."

Miranda left well enough alone. She waited while Janey dug in a box, extracting bits and pieces before arranging them on the bench. Miranda recognized a tank of aether much like the ones at her father's airfield.

Janey swiftly fit the pieces together, assembling a rifle. All the while, she cast anxious glances at Miranda from beneath the fringe of blond hair that fell into her eyes. Up until now, Mrs. Randall had been their go-between. This was their first real conversation alone.

"I'm glad you came," Janey said. "I didn't want to go any further until I knew this was what you were looking for."

"All right," Miranda agreed, curious about the maker. Although her speech was educated, the young woman's accent said she was from the hard-working district near the docks. Perhaps she had attended one of the charity schools that sprang up in such places.

Janey held up the contraption. "You see, I made a few amendments to your plan."

Miranda balked inside, but then saw how Janey had improved her design. "You added a sight."

"I did. And I made the nozzle easier to clean. That's the big problem with these weapons—they choke too easily." Janey held out the gun for Miranda's consideration. The workmanship was beautiful, the metal scrolled with ornate designs. It was an unexpected touch of finesse.

"Where did you learn to do such exquisite work?" Miranda asked.

"My mother," Janey replied with a shrug. "She was an engraver."

"I'm in awe."

That made Janey smile. "And here's something else. With a weapon this compact, the aether cylinder has to be small. A small aether supply means the charge won't last long. That's no good, so I made the cylinders interchangeable."

"How does that work?"

Janey pointed to the small brass tube on the side. "You can unscrew it and put another one on whenever you need to, even if the gun is hot."

"That's an excellent idea." Miranda was truly impressed.

Janey blinked with pleasure, holding her creation out to Miranda. "See how it feels."

It felt perfect. The weight and balance were exactly right. The size fit her frame. This was a weapon she could carry and shoot for long stretches without starting to ache. "I'd love to try it out."

Grinning, Janey handed her a pair of tinted goggles. "You'll want these. It makes quite a flash."

After struggling to strap on the goggles, Miranda made a mental note to simplify her hairdo for combat. Then she followed Janey outside to where a target had been painted on the old brick wall beside the alley. Miranda lifted the rifle and took aim, realizing how good a job Janey had done of making precision simple. When she squeezed gently, the weapon made a slight hiss as a ball of activated aether flew and struck the target dead center. Chips of brick flew.

"Excellent," Miranda said.

Janey nodded in satisfaction. "You're a good shot, miss. I didn't expect it, seeing as you don't need to shoot for a living."

No, thought Miranda, *but I may need to shoot to stay alive.* "My father's an airman."

"Oh, I know that," Janey said. "So was mine, but he was nowhere near so famous."

"If you do work like this, you could have a job with my father in a minute," Miranda said.

Janey shook her head, a stubborn tilt to her pointed chin. "That's a kind offer, miss, but I'm used to my freedom."

"Now you *sound* like my father," Miranda said with a laugh.

She raised the gun again, ready to take a second shot, but the trigger only clicked with a wheeze from the barrel. Lowering it, she gave the rifle a curious look.

Janey swore under her breath. "It does that after one or two shots."

"Is it the nozzle?"

"No." Janey took the rifle back. "It's something to do with the aether passing through the coil. It leaves a sticky film."

Miranda remembered her conversation with Kitteridge. "I know someone who might have a solution to that."

Of course, that meant braving the perils of his library.

CHAPTER 13

According to the Society page of the newspaper, Kitteridge was staying at his grandfather's looming mansion, The Willows. Armed with that information, Miranda copied Mrs. Randall's bold method of sending an anonymous invitation to meet at the Mercury Café. Subterfuge was necessary since genteel young ladies did not summon gentlemen in such fashion—but after visiting a notorious brothel, the breach of propriety seemed almost incidental.

She requested a meeting for the next day. When the time of the appointment drew near, the late afternoon had turned rainy. Miranda used her umbrella and heavy coat as elements of her disguise. She opted for a dark blue dress with little jewelry, making herself as unremarkable as she could. It was also the closest she had to mourning clothes without actually wearing black. While she would not accept that Sidonie dead until she'd seen evidence of it, she still needed to recognize her loss, whatever Councilor Ormond said.

What would Sidonie think about meeting Kitteridge like this? Miranda wondered as the curricle rumbled down the street. Her sister had always been a lady, but never a coward. There had been the incident with the rowboat and the one with the Christmas guests—the Towlands still weren't on speaking terms. And she'd hidden Madam Alma in the attic.

True, Sidonie might encourage Miranda to take Olivia along as a chaperone, but that would put yet another of her sisters in peril. Papa needed to have one child safe, in case the worst happened. Miranda couldn't be that selfish, even for her own safety.

The sky was darkening when she arrived a deliberate five minutes late. To her disappointment, Kitteridge wasn't there. She had wanted to use the delay to observe her quarry and be sure of her approach. Unfortunately, and embarrassingly, it seemed he had ignored her request. She swore bitterly in the privacy of her heart.

Miranda turned to leave, and nearly ran headlong into a tall figure in a gray alpaca coat. "Mr. Kitteridge," she said, breathless with surprise. "There you are."

"Was I missing?" he asked pleasantly.

She took a step back. "You startled me."

"I prefer to astonish, but one must begin somewhere."

"Very well, consider my amazement initiated."

He held out a hand. "I presume you are my mystery correspondent."

"If I confess, how shall I preserve an air of suspense?"

"I'm sure you'll think of something."

"Thank you." She allowed him to escort her to a table set in a discreet back corner. "And thank you for accepting my invitation."

He held her chair as she sat. "I recall inviting you to view my library, but this will do."

"I have a reputation to maintain," Miranda said.

"And libraries are dangerous." He gave a lift of his dark brows. "So many covers to be lifted. So many pages turned." His smile was pure sin.

Miranda flushed. "I'm not in the mood for mockery."

He instantly sobered. "Of course. I'm so sorry. I'm well aware your family is experiencing a difficult time."

He might have been sincere, but it was hard to tell with such a man. In his defense, he had sent a beautiful hothouse bouquet.

"Thank you for the flowers," she said.

"Poor comfort, I know."

Miranda's mouth had gone dry. She was reminded again of how extraordinarily handsome Kitteridge was, with his tumble of jet-black locks and sooty eyelashes. He had a perfect nose and a slightly cleft chin, as if his face had been the product of a sculptor's quest for an ideal.

"To what do I owe the honor of this invitation?" he asked. "I suspect it involves more than charming banter."

"I require your advice," she said.

His eyes widened. "Indeed? Something tells me that I shall need fortification." He turned to a passing waiter, then placed an order for wine.

"First, I require your promise of discretion," Miranda said.

He dipped his chin. "I assure you, Miss Fletcher, I am as discreet as the grave."

"Then as long as the tomb door remains firmly sealed, we shall not have difficulties," she said, allowing a tart edge to creep into her words. "No revenants, please."

He held up a hand. "Not one tiny ghoul."

The server, who was just delivering the wine, gave a questioning glance at the words. Unrepentant, Kitteridge took the bottle from his hand and poured.

Once they were alone again, Miranda described her rifle and Janey's difficulties. As he listened, Kitteridge's expression moved from polite interest to intense concentration.

When she had finished, he inclined his head. "I came to this rendezvous expecting quite a different conversation. You are not like other ladies, Miss Fletcher."

Miranda gave a slight shrug. "I may have some interests that coincide with yours, but that is hardly the definition of extraordinary."

He put his chin in his hand. "If I were to woo you with poems and moonlight walks, would you succumb to my charms?"

He picked up the bottle with his free hand, then topped off her glass.

"Probably," she said blithely, "but I have some monsters to kill first."

He straightened, genuinely alarmed. "Excuse me?"

Miranda froze. She hadn't meant to disclose her plans quite so freely, but the wine and witty conversation had loosened her tongue. She considered Kitteridge, reading the lines of his face and the tension in his body. There was no question he enjoyed the usual vices of a rich young man with too little to do, but he craved excitement. That was something else they shared.

"In all honesty," she said, "and although I might be mocked for saying so, our servants were not attacked by wolves. To the best of my knowledge, wolves do not engage in abduction."

Kitteridge exhaled slowly, sitting forward in his chair. "That is a very alarming assertion, Miss Fletcher."

He slid his hand forward, his fingers touching hers. Gaslights glowed outside, but inside the café was lit only by the pools of candlelight on the tables. There was a hushed stillness the murmur of conversation could not disturb.

His gaze held hers, all flirtation gone. "Putting together the fact you are designing this weapon, and your problems are more than shaggy dogs, I can only surmise that you intend to go hunting."

"That is a reasonable assumption," Miranda said.

"Please don't. I won't sleep at night."

"Someone has taken my eldest sister. What if they come for another member of my family?"

"They?"

"Our not-wolves. This is not the first disappearance I have heard about, nor is it the first attack. There are a thousand unanswered questions about these cases, and where I have been able to learn any detail—and I freely admit reliable accounts are rare —these not-wolves are the common element."

"And, to stretch the metaphor, removing dangerous wildlife from the local forest is a logical first step?" Kitteridge asked.

"Perhaps. I don't see an alternative."

She spoke the words before she'd consciously formed the thought. It was all theory, of course, easy to say when she was sitting safe and drinking wine. And yet, nothing happened without intention. There was a reason she was building her weapon.

Kitteridge closed his fingers around hers. There was nothing suggestive in it—he seemed genuinely concerned.

"In case you're wondering," she said, "I'm an excellent shot."

Kitteridge withdrew his hand and laced his fingers together, almost in an attitude of prayer. "The thing with these predators is they are more dangerous when wounded. One must shoot them squarely in the head or the heart."

Her breath caught in relief. He was willing to give her real information. "That is precisely what I need to know."

"Where did you come from, Miranda Fletcher?" he asked, seeming almost angry. "Where does a schoolgirl—come, don't frown; you are hardly a seasoned campaigner in life—suddenly gain the audacity for such a fight?"

"I mean to find my sister," she said simply. "I'm not a mage or a brilliant scientist, so I must work with what talents I have. I can shoot and fly a ship."

He narrowed his eyes, suddenly cool. "You're throwing down your life like a bravo spoiling for a duel."

Miranda's pulse sped up. Why did this man, of all people, see her so clearly? She slowly raised her chin. "Are you going to stop me?"

He sat back with a sigh, running his hands through his hair. "Heavens, no. I'm far too indolent to tie you up and take you back to your father."

"What a relief." She sipped her wine.

"If you have the enterprise to design and build an aether rifle, I'm not silly enough to interfere. I don't fancy having it turned on me." Kitteridge tossed back the rest of his drink, then paused a long moment before he spoke again. "Your maker is using the wrong grade of aether. The weight used on dirigibles is relatively crude. The concentrate used for weapons requires a different distillation process."

Miranda sat forward. "Go on."

"Unfortunately, the conventional weapons-grade brew is notoriously unstable. Drop the canister and you're likely to become your own projectile." His smile was wry. "Trust me on that point."

"Even with a high-grade mixture?"

"Any that your maker could obtain."

"I did not realize that was the case."

"It always was, until now. That's why most professionals still prefer to use standard firearms. I studied the problem quite extensively while I was at Stonegate."

"At the university?"

"Indeed."

There was something evasive in the one word, as if his education were only a small part of the story, but it was none of her business. "Go on."

"There is another level of refinement necessary to stabilize the compressed matter once it's ready to be loaded into the typical firearms cylinder."

"Does any of that prevent clogging inside the feeder coil?"

"Yes, but the process is a secret known only to a handful of researchers at the moment."

Miranda was enough her father's daughter to understand the

economic potential of such a breakthrough. "Are you authorized to share this with me?"

"Absolutely not, but then you've trusted me with a detailed description of your rifle design. Now your naiveté is balanced with my indiscretion. We have each other's secrets, tit for tat."

Her heart skipped a beat. This conversation felt much like that long walk along the aqueducts, with no rail to save her from a deadly drop in the dark. "And where did you come from, Mr. William Kitteridge? What fate threw you in my path?"

He dipped his head, the candlelight modeling his cheekbones. Really, he was so attractive it was nearly indecent. Miranda allowed herself another restorative sip of wine.

"I came to be as everyone does," Kitteridge said, "with precious little say in the process. I owe my grandfather a great deal for trying to make a good man out of me. If there is a medal for such things, he surely deserves it."

That made her smile.

"Where is your maker located?" he asked.

"Hellion House."

He regarded her with unmitigated shock. "However did you come to know those ladies?"

"It was serendipity," she said. "Though of a most unpleasant kind. A tale for another day."

He chuckled. "I won't rest until I have that story."

Miranda blessed the gloom hiding her burning cheeks. She hadn't meant to continue their association—not consciously, at least. "And how do you know about Hellion House, even though you've been in our town for barely a quarter of an hour?"

"You stretch the facts abominably. I've been here nearly a month."

"I've heard you were a rake."

His mouth curled in a half smile. "I seem to be with everyone but you."

"And why deprive me?"

He lifted her hand from the table, pressing a kiss to her glove. His lips were warm even through the barrier of the butter-soft kid. The sensation tingled to the base of her spine.

"Mr. Kitteridge," she said, withdrawing her hand. "Do not mistake my intentions. I came for information, not an assignation. This is not the beginning of a love affair."

His smile showed the tips of his teeth. "I would not presume."

But he would, given the least chance. They both knew it, and it was time to put an end to the interview. She rose, gathering her reticule. "Thank you so much for your advice."

He stood as well, placing one hand to the shining buttons of his coat. "Aim for the head and heart, little huntress, in death *and* in love."

"Good evening, Mr. Kitteridge."

"Good evening, Miss Fletcher. I dream of once again finding myself in your sights."

CHAPTER 14

Afternoon light slanted low across the Grove of Angels. Miranda walked between the graves, looking at the same ground she'd paced a thousand times. The search for Sidonie was officially over, though the family quietly carried on. Gideon and Miranda had come that day, along with Dr. Wilcox. Gideon wandered the grounds, but the doctor sat on a stone bench under a cypress tree, his expression weary and his hands dangling between his knees. Concerned, Miranda sat beside him.

"My great-grandfather came to Londria to find adventure," he said. "He was a physician, too. A pioneer of many techniques. He took a risk, leaving his quiet home a continent away, but he was willing to trade comfort for greater opportunity."

"The gamble paid off, didn't it?" Miranda asked, unsure where the conversation was going.

"To most eyes, yes. We have influence. Fortune." He bowed his head.

"And?"

"What good is it? Fortune doesn't buy safety. It doesn't buy concern from those meant to protect us." He raised his head to meet Miranda's gaze. Anger sharpened the line of his jaw. "Now my wife—for she was almost that, wasn't she?—has become a report on someone's shelf. No, a footnote—easy to erase and forget. I wonder, beneath the fine clothes and polite conversation, if there is a difference between this city's potentates and the very devils of hell."

Miranda squeezed his hand. "Do you mind if I ask you a question?"

He pulled off his top hat, rubbing his closely cropped head. "No."

"What happened at Hellion House after Gideon and I left?"

His dark eyes studied her. "Why do you ask?"

"Consider it simple curiosity."

"You shouldn't have been there to begin with."

"But I was," she replied. "Nothing will keep me safer than knowing what we're up against."

Need for information was the one thing guaranteed to sway the doctor. He grimaced, but gave in.

"The guards searched the place—or a search is what they called it. In truth, it was an excuse to frighten the women into silence. They promised consequences if we breathed a word about the attack."

He made a fist. Suddenly alarmed, Miranda wondered what threats they'd used against him. She knew him well, but not well enough to ask.

"Then they took Tupper's body, and left." Wilcox made a helpless gesture. "Whatever we might have learned from his injuries left with him."

After a minute of strained silence, Miranda left the doctor with his thoughts. She needed to pace, to walk off her restless energy. Anger simmered so hot it felt as if her skin should be glowing with it.

Mere months ago, Londria had seemed good to her. She'd

been aware of the dangers beyond the barrier, but none of that darkness had touched her life. Official silence had shrouded any unpleasantness from the morning paper or conversations over tea.

The deception made her livid, but acting on her anger was another matter, despite her brave words to Kitteridge. What could she, Miranda, do in the face of creatures like Ormond—much less the literal monsters? Her only certainty was that she couldn't ignore the facts.

If only she was certain what those were. She had scraps, but not a complete picture.

After a few minutes' walk, she spied a burial in progress a short distance away, with a scatter of family members looking on. A twinge of jealousy flashed through her. At least they knew what had become of their loved one.

To her surprise, she saw her brother among the mourners, talking to Councilor Ormond. They stood apart from the funeral party, heads bent in conversation. The sight filled her with confusion. Why were they together? Was the councilor lecturing Gideon the way he had Miranda and her father? That wasn't a welcome thought—since the attack, Gideon's temper had been on a hair trigger. He'd likely say something dreadful.

Miranda circled the trees, hoping to eavesdrop.

"I'm here as a friend of the family," Ormond was saying to Gideon. "The Conclave leaves religion to the priests."

There was a faint note of contempt in his voice. Miranda held her breath as she found a position behind a yew hedge, close enough to hear but screened from view by the thick green branches.

"I hope you will forgive my intrusion," Gideon replied, his tone surprisingly polite. "I only require an instant of your time, but you may know the answer to a troubling question."

"Indeed?" Ormond sounded doubtful.

"If the Conclave leaves religion to the priests, what is their position on law enforcement?"

Miranda's breath caught. Gideon knew the answer as well as she did. The Citadel trumped Londria's laws at every turn.

"I don't understand," Ormond replied.

"Where are Inspector Palmer's men? Shouldn't they be here today?"

There was a beat of silence where Miranda didn't breathe.

When he replied, Ormond was almost fatherly. "You must realize this area has been exhaustively searched without results, and there are other investigations that require attention. If any new evidence comes to light, Inspector Palmer will be sure to pursue it."

Miranda wondered how the inspector felt about being told to stand down.

"What about my sister?" Gideon demanded—loudly.

Alarmed, Miranda shifted to see through the hedge. People from the burial were glancing over.

"As I said to your father, there is a time for all things, and the time for grief is drawing to a close." Ormond's voice was suffused with a sympathetic note Miranda did not believe.

"Why? Is it better to change the conversation than admit we failed her?"

Gideon was skirting dangerously close to an accusation. Miranda shifted her weight, ready to lunge through the hedge and create a distraction. Anything to shut him up.

Ormond's sigh was audible. "Your sister was a lovely girl. Don't do something in her name you will later regret."

Cursing, Gideon tore his hat from his head and ran a hand through his dark hair. Miranda began to move, but froze as he spun on his heel and stalked away, muttering under his breath. The sudden departure broke the charged atmosphere like lightning, making her shiver. Without a flicker of emotion, Ormond returned to the burial, his step unhurried.

Miranda turned away from the hedge, limp with the release of tension. There was no point in going after Gideon. He would be a bear until he had time to cool off. She returned to the bench where Dr. Wilcox still sat.

As she approached, a boy—not Billy—arrived with a summons for the doctor from Hellion House. One of the women was about to give birth, and the delivery was expected to be more than the midwife could manage.

"Take me with you," Miranda pleaded.

Wilcox looked shocked. "Whatever for?"

After hours of anxious frustration, she needed to do something useful. She could seize this opportunity to view Janey's progress on the aether weapon. However, she wasn't about to discuss her project with the doctor. She needed a different excuse.

"One of the ladies of the house wishes to learn some basic bandaging skills. You don't need to spend time on simple instruction. I can share what I've learned at father's airfield."

It was a comment on the doctor's exhaustion that he believed her.

When Miranda reached the shed behind Hellion House, dusk was approaching. An ear-splitting noise rang from the tiny building, like metal tearing in two. Curious, she pushed open the door.

Janey was working the foot pedal of a contraption made of cables and whirring gears. When Miranda peered more closely, she saw it was a clockwork screwdriver fastening tiny bolts into a large brass disk. It looked like a shield for a gigantic Viking. Janey lifted her head, removing her foot from the pedal. The gears whirred to a stop, leaving blessed silence.

"Hello, miss," Janey said with a grin.

"What is that?" Miranda asked.

"I'm making it for a gentleman who believes he can transmit messages through the air. It's a reception disk for invisible words. I think he's quite mad, but he pays well."

"I see." Miranda was dubious, but she'd seen strange things in her short life.

Janey hopped off her stool. "I have brilliant news. Someone delivered a canister of aether distillate far finer than anything I've ever seen before."

"Fancy that." Miranda closed the door, careful of who heard this part of the conversation.

"I wish I knew who it was. I'd send our benefactor a cake." Janey took the gun from its case, then handed it to Miranda.

Miranda was considering whether to mention Kitteridge's name, but all such thoughts fled when she saw the weapon. It had been a beautiful piece before, but Janey had lavished even more attention on it. Miranda raised it in one swift movement, admiring its perfect balance.

"Please don't pull the trigger inside the workshop, miss," Janey said. "I've been using too many chemicals to risk firing a shot."

"I suppose you like your roof where it is."

"It's a consideration."

Miranda lowered the weapon. "Shall we go try it?"

"For certain," Janey said. "Just hang on a tick while I put this aside."

Miranda set the gun down before helping Janey move the large copper disk against the wall.

"Janey," Miranda said, choosing her words carefully, "I understand when Councilor Ormond and his guards came to remove Mr. Tupper's body, there were threats against this house."

"There were," Janey replied, grunting as they shifted the heavy weight.

"Did they say specifically what they'd do?"

"Not in plain words, but it was clear we'd see the inside of the House of Questions." Janey swore as she heaved the disk the last few inches into place. Metal scraped as it came to rest against the workbench. "They were looking for something when they searched the house. A few of the guards were just smashing things, but Ormond was looking in drawers and closets. He didn't find what he was after. I think if he had, he would have grabbed it and burned the rest to the ground."

Miranda's stomach went cold. "Do you know what that was?"

"I don't. We're just ordinary folks making a living. We kept Madam Alma's things out here, in my jumble, but what would a man like Ormond want with fortune-teller's gear?"

It was a good question, especially since Miranda had some of that gear under the floorboards of her bedroom.

They were dusting off their hands when Janey frowned. "Do you hear that?"

Miranda fell silent to listen. There was an odd scratching sound, like a creature digging outside the door. "Rats? A dog?"

She knew that was wrong even as she said it. Something about the sound was out of place. Janey peered out the shed's small window, but then the noise stopped. Shrugging, she returned to where Miranda was cleaning her hands on a rag. A moment later, the scratching was back.

This time, they both turned toward the sound and gasped. Something was working its way through the wall. They stared in astonishment, but then Miranda drew nearer to see what on earth was wriggling its way in.

Claw-tipped fingers, like pale bones come to life, worked through the old planks. Miranda hopped back with a sound of revulsion. Janey picked up a hooked blade from the bench, springing forward to slash at the claws. The hand was snatched back, followed by a horrible gurgling squeal.

"That'll teach 'em," Janey said with a growl, but her face had gone white.

A second later, a fist burst through the window, shattering the glass. The two women scrambled away. Miranda grabbed the edge of the table, flipping it onto its side to make a barricade. Tools and shreds of metal scattered across the floor unheeded.

They ducked just as the Unseen's shaggy head pushed through the broken window, oblivious to the razor-sharp glass. Miranda peered over the edge of the table as the creature forced an arm, then a shoulder, and then the rest of its body through the opening, wriggling through until slid it to the floor like a serpent. It got to all fours, sniffing the air.

The upturned table lay in front of the workbench, forming a protective cave. Janey trembled, her eyes wide, but Miranda's senses sharpened, as if terror were a stimulant drug.

The Unseen crawled across the floor, sputtering and sneezing at the strong odors of the workshop. Perhaps the smell of grease and aether would confuse it for a minute, but it wouldn't be long before it found them. Miranda reached up, running her fingers across the old, scarred wood of the workbench until she found Janey's spanner. It was as heavy as a cudgel. Miranda silently drew it down to their hiding place, where Janey took it from her hand.

The creature grew impatient, snuffling back and forth and muttering to itself. Clearly, its eyesight—at least in daylight—wasn't as good as its nose. A useful fact to know.

Miranda needed a weapon of her own—one that wouldn't cause an explosion. She reached up again, feeling her way along the bench as she had before. This time, her fingers found a ragged shred of metal that sliced her thumb open. Hot pain made her start, then she felt the sticky sensation of blood. The Unseen swiveled with a grunt of satisfaction, its nose working as it caught the coppery scent. The game was up.

Miranda surged from behind the table, grabbing at the clockwork screwdriver Janey had been using before. She stomped on the pedal, setting the gears in motion. The whine of the mechanism was earsplitting, and the creature clutched at its head, letting forth a pained howl. Breathless with panic, Miranda pumped the pedal until the gears blurred with speed.

The Unseen leaped just as she thrust the sharp tip forward. The creature collided with the spinning point, jolting Miranda backward as it all but skewered itself. Her back slammed into the edge of the bench, forcing her to lean back from the Unseen's slashing nails. As it scraped her collar, she felt the horrible tickle of the razor-sharp points.

Janey jumped up from her hiding place, clobbering it with the spanner. With a confused squawk, the creature lurched for safety, crashing through the litter of debris and yowling as its feet met shards of broken glass.

Its rush led it to the window, and it wriggled out the same way it had entered. A glance through the smashed pane showed it loping across the scrubby grass.

Miranda sagged against the wall, barely able to hold herself upright. Now that the skirmish was over, she was panting and shaking, more frightened than she thought possible.

"We got it," Janey said, wiping sweat from her brow. She was still pale, but her eyes snapped with affronted fury. "It won't be back."

"Where did it go?"

Janey cracked the door open to take a cautious peek. Her shoulders hunched. "It's heading for the house."

Miranda swore softly. There was a woman having a baby in that house. Chasing the Unseen from the workshop wasn't good enough. She straightened, picked up the aether gun, and pushed the door fully open.

The purple light of dusk erased detail from the garden. Rocky ground crunched beneath Miranda's heels as she left the safety of the workshop, the rifle a comforting weight in her hand. She could see movement near the kitchen window as the creature sought handholds to climb the back of Hellion House. Miranda took another step, wishing the light was better. She took aim as it glanced over its shoulder, its face a pale circle in the gloom.

All movement stopped as it focused on her. When she met its

eyes, they were sharp, glittering points in the dusk. All she saw there was hunger.

Miranda fired, closing her eyes against the blinding flash. A faint *shush* sounded as the ball released, then she heard the crunch and sizzle of flesh. The sound seemed to shudder along her spine. She lowered the weapon, suddenly dizzy with nerves.

The creature was down. Even from a distance, Miranda knew it would not rise again. Nausea rushed in, leaving her sticky with sweat. She staggered back a step, fighting an urge to vomit.

Janey came up beside her. "You didn't even try the rifle first."

She sucked in a breath. "Take it as faith in your workmanship."

Janey put an arm around her as they went to see what the gun had done. It had obliterated most of the creature's chest, leaving a charred, smoking ruin. Pale shards of bone stuck out from the gore.

"Bloody hell," Janey murmured.

"We have to tell somebody," Miranda said, dragging her mind from the destruction. "Now we have hard evidence the Unseen are in the city."

Janey spun to face her. "No."

Miranda blinked. "But surely—"

"No." Janey was emphatic. "Didn't I tell you what Ormond and his like will do to Hellion House? To Mrs. Randall and all of us here if word gets out that we said anything?"

"But that was about Tupper."

Janey pointed at the bloody corpse. "Maybe that's what killed the poor sod. We have to hide the remains."

"But it's evidence," Miranda said just as urgently. "We can't pretend this didn't happen, or people will keep dying. Or they'll go missing."

Janey ducked her chin. "I understand why you want to tell the world, but this is my home. We won't be safe if we make this public."

Janey was right. Miranda turned her back on the bloody mess at her feet. "There's got to be a compromise."

And they didn't have long to find one. A birth in progress would distract the residents of the house for a while, but sooner or later someone would notice the carnage in the garden. Janey shifted nervously, as if she might bolt. Then her face lit up. "I have an idea."

She ran toward the workshop, arms pumping. Seconds later, she came back with a large black box bound with brass hinges. The return trip was slower as the box seemed heavy. When she reached Miranda's side again, she set it down with care.

"What is that?" Miranda asked.

Instead of replying, Janey popped a handle from the side of the cube and began cranking it. The box raised up an inch at a time as a tripod pushed out from the base. When she was satisfied with the height, Janey unlatched the sides of the box. They dropped away to reveal an expensive-looking camera.

"Some of the ladies here find use for a portrait or two," Janey said with a sideways glance.

Miranda carefully kept her mind on the job at hand. "Why take a picture if you want to keep this a secret?"

"The body fell on the grass. If I cut everything else out of the frame, who can say where the picture was taken? You get your evidence. I protect the house."

"Then how does that prove the Unseen was inside the city?"

Janey gave a mirthless laugh. "Who takes a camera into the forest? You'd be eaten before you unlatched the case."

That was true enough. "And then what?"

"We anonymously send prints to anyone who matters."

"Not anonymously."

"What do you mean?" Janey said, her voice cautious.

Miranda looked down at the weapon in her hand. She hadn't enjoyed killing—not at all—but she'd kept the Unseen from reaching the house. The woman and her baby and all the other innocent lives were safe. That didn't help Sidonie, but she'd still done something that mattered.

And once the truth was out, not even Councilor Ormond could stop it. Miranda met Janey's worried eyes.

"The picture will be courtesy of the Scorpion."

CHAPTER 15

"A parcel came for you, miss."

Miranda glanced up to see her maid, Shore, standing in the doorway. The girl held a large package under her arm. It looked like a dress box, but Miranda wasn't expecting anything from the *modiste*.

"Set it on the bed," she said, not particularly interested in new gowns at the moment.

Her mind was on the Unseen she'd shot at Hellion House. Janey had anonymously distributed the photographs three days ago, but there hadn't been a word about the incident in the papers. Someone was burying the evidence of the attack. What should the Scorpion's next step be?

"Miss?" Shore prompted, obviously more curious than Miranda was about the parcel.

Hiding her impatience, Miranda crossed to the bed. "Who is it from?"

"It doesn't say."

Finally intrigued, Miranda searched for a return address. There was nothing. Had it come from Hellion House? Mrs. Randall was known for sending mysterious letters, but nothing about the package implied that lady's touch. Perhaps it had come from Janey? There was a no-nonsense appearance she'd expect from the maker. Whatever the case, this was a mystery to explore in private.

"Shore," she said, "be so kind as to run down to the kitchen for some of Mrs. Trencher's blackberry cordial. I fancy a glass."

Shore regarded her with naked curiosity. The drink was no one's favorite, and Mrs. Trencher had been receiving alternative recipes beneath the sitting room door for years. But a good servant knew better than to question her mistress, and so, after bobbing a curtsy, Shore left.

Miranda pulled a pair of scissors from her work basket. Once she'd cut the string on the box, she lifted the lid. Beneath a light layer of muslin lay a high leather collar studded with brass, perfect for guarding one's throat against fangs. Beneath that was a heavy leather coat. Miranda held it up, a quick scan assuring her it would be a good fit. The garment was beautiful, form and function in perfect balance.

The leather was walnut brown and supple as a glove, but much thicker. Transfixed, she stepped before her looking glass, holding up the coat to study the effect. It was not designed to wear over petticoats and a bustle. The seams followed the curve of her body almost indecently, but there would be an excellent range of movement where needed. Paired with an airman's trousers and boots, she could run and climb as freely as a man. Miranda turned to study herself from another angle. She liked this version of herself, practical but still elegant.

A movement outside her door broke the spell. It sounded like Olivia hurrying toward the stairs, but the disturbance brought Miranda back to immediate problems. Until she knew more about this unexpected delivery, she preferred to keep it to herself,

She hid the garments in the bottom of her blanket chest, where Shore seldom looked. Then she lifted the muslin lining from the delivery box, intending to fold it, but an envelope hidden beneath it caught her attention. It was plain, bearing nothing but "Miss F" in a man's angular scrawl. She broke the wax seal and slid out a piece of writing paper.

My dear Miss Fletcher,

Accept these poor offerings as a token of my esteem. Please do let me know how you get on.

K.

Kitteridge. A flush heated Miranda's cheeks. This was the man all over, putting her in an indelicate position. How could she keep these offerings, poor or otherwise? A lady could not accept personal gifts from gentlemen who were not her relation. Besides, what sort of a thank-you note would one write for a suit of monster-killing armor?

With a sad pang, she wondered what quip Sidonie would make right then. Her sister would see the humor in Miranda's position, even as she understood the dire need for the leather garments—and what accepting them might do to Miranda's good name.

But Sidonie was gone, and this was Miranda's decision to make.

She was keeping the armor. She would need it. That meant dealing with Kitteridge again, and probably soon. She owed him for the armor and the aether, too.

How much did he expect in return? An excellent—and uncomfortable—question.

Miranda folded his letter and placed it in the bottom of her drawer, alongside Mrs. Randall's missives. She had other questions about Kitteridge, about how he had materialized just when she needed someone with his skills. The man was a puzzle and a problem, but one Miranda hoped would stay in town—at least for a while.

Shore returned with a tray holding a glass and a crystal decanter. The beautiful deep shade of the cordial was alluring, but Miranda already knew it was at odds with the noxious taste. Nevertheless, after Shore set the tray down, Miranda filled a glass. She needed a drink.

"Miss?" Shore asked. "Is everything all right?"

"Yes, of course," she lied.

A plan was gathering shape. It was going to be a long night.

DETECTIVE INSPECTOR PALMER'S office was in the center of the city, half-a-dozen blocks from the Citadel. The law courts and parliament were close by, as well as the administrative offices for everything from street sweepers to the tax collectors.

Palmer's station stood at the end of the street, a little apart from the other buildings as if none of its fellows wished to call it friend. It was solid but shabby, its square silhouette guarding the corner like a bulldog.

Gideon arrived just after noon, dawdling a moment on the sidewalk to consider his approach. He was there to demand Palmer keep searching for Sidonie. Justice was the foundation of public order, and there could be no justice if the police simply shrugged and gave in to devils like Ormond.

Beneath that logic lay more personal reasons. Sidonie was his twin. There were years of loving and squabbling and pulling together in the face of the adult world. And there was brotherly love for the woman Sidonie had become. Such things were hard to put into words.

Including his conviction that Sidonie still lived. Twins were bonded from the womb. He would know if she had left the earth, and nothing would be over until she was found.

He had failed to save her. He wouldn't do so again. Adjusting his hat, Gideon mounted the worn stone steps to the front door. A statue of Athena stood to one side of the double doors, Hercules to the other. Wisdom and strength. Gideon wasn't sure either had been present in Londria lately.

The doors flew open and a handful of uniformed officers ran down the steps, parting to pass by Gideon's either side. They barely spared him a glance, obviously intent on a mission.

He went inside. Chaos engulfed the main counter facing the door. Behind the scarred oak barrier, two older officers shouted orders at the milling crush of police and public. Gideon scanned the surroundings, noting a stairway to the right and a door to more offices to the left. Unsure which way to go, he pushed his way through the crowd.

"Where is Inspector Palmer?" he shouted above the din.

One of the officers behind the desk gave him a brief glance, but got distracted when someone in the crowd threw a punch. Realizing he would get no help, Gideon turned toward the stairs.

Beyond the front foyer, the building was dim and in need of a thorough scrubbing. A strange smell permeated the stairwell, reminding him of old tea and dirty feet. And yet the place was oddly thrilling. People worked hard here to solve urgent problems. The risks and rewards were real.

He pushed through the door to the second floor and down the corridor, reading the names stenciled on the office doors. Finding no sign of the inspector, he went up to the third floor, which was even less well kept.

There, he found his quarry. Palmer sat behind a desk, a mound of paper in front of him. Gideon knocked on the open door before entering. Palmer set down his pen, then leaned back in his chair. If he was surprised to see Gideon, it didn't show.

"What can I do for you, Mr. Fletcher?" he said, folding his hands behind his head. "You realize this is a restricted area? The public isn't allowed to go wandering on these floors."

"It's a madhouse downstairs."

"It's the day the river workers get paid. Their wages go straight to the taverns."

Of course. Everything the city couldn't produce had to come by air or water, and no vessel was completely safe from the Unseen. Great coal barges sailed into the river port twice a week, guarded by the roughest mercenaries that gold could buy. The days when those men got drunk brought mayhem to the streets.

"Why are you here, Mr. Fletcher?" Palmer asked again.

"Why has the search for Sidonie ended?"

"Orders," Palmer replied. "We've been assigned to other cases."

It was what Ormond had said, but it made no more sense coming from the inspector. "What could be more important than finding my sister?"

Sadness flickered across Palmer's face. "Other people's sisters. Other people's sons and daughters and wives and husbands. People we might have a chance of finding. It's a nasty chaotic world, and more people than you might think vanish without a trace."

"Still, you've got knowledge, weapons, personnel. Are you saying there's no hope of finding her?"

"After three weeks, the chances are slim. I'm honestly sorry, but there's just not enough of us to keep going."

Gideon believed him, which didn't help his mood. But something Palmer had said gave Gideon an opening. "If it's manpower you need, let me provide it. I will keep looking myself. I can bring others in. We can be your arms and legs if you provide the proper methods and techniques."

"It doesn't work that way," Palmer replied, opening a cigarette case and offering it to Gideon.

Gideon shook his head, but he waited while Palmer lit a cheroot with his dragon lighter.

"Police work must be done by police officers," Palmer added. "I can't put the heir to the Fletcher fortune in harm's way. Not on official business. If something happened to you, the grief would rain down so hard this whole station would float out to sea."

"Please." Uninvited, Gideon sat in the rickety chair across from Palmer's desk. When the chair groaned, Gideon made sure to sit still. "I've tried looking on my own but I'm having no luck. Tell me how to succeed."

Palmer held up a hand to still Gideon's words. "The only way to learn this work is by doing it. The only way to be good is to give up every other distraction. It's not a pastime for gentlemen."

"I'm not a gentleman."

A smile more like a grimace creased Palmer's face. "Have you actually worked a day in your life?"

"I've flown at least a hundred rescue missions beyond the wall. I've seen my share of scrapes."

Palmer's expression didn't change, but his shoulders relaxed a fraction. "Have you considered becoming an inquiry agent?"

"Will it get my sister back?"

"It might help."

A flicker of hope—a sensation he'd feared lost forever—made him straighten. "By inquiry agent, do you mean a detective for hire?"

"Private agents operate independently of the police. They have no official authority. Then again, they have no leash either. They are not forced to abandon cases on a whim."

Gideon sat forward. The chair protested his weight, and he stilled again. "I'm interested."

"There's little money in it," Palmer warned, "but I suppose that's not a concern for you."

"I just want my sister back. How does this private inquiry business help with that?"

"You keep looking for your sister. In the meantime, you build your skills by working on other cases."

"Like what?"

"Cases I can't touch." Palmer slid a picture from under the pile of papers on his desk. He turned it around, then pushed it toward Gideon.

His heart leaped. It was a photograph—or part of one—featuring an Unseen sprawled across the grass, most of its chest blown away. "Where did this come from?"

The photograph had been half-burned. There was a partial line printed on the back. *A gift from* was all that remained.

"They've been appearing all over town. We've been ordered to burn every copy and pretend it never existed. I picked that out of the ash."

"Does someone else have a complete copy?"

"Undoubtedly, but no one will admit to it. Almost no one confesses to having seen it in the first place."

"What do you want me to do?"

"Find out where it came from," Palmer said. "I'm not sure if I'll shake the photographer's hand or throw him in a cell, but I want the story of that picture."

Gideon nodded. Someone else had seen the monsters inside the city. That was worth something. "How do I start?"

"By thinking," Palmer said. "This is dangerous work, so take a day or two to consider the matter. Then, if you're still eager for my advice, I might give it."

"I won't change my mind."

"Then I will expect a return visit." Palmer picked up his pen, grabbed a form, and began filling it out. "In the meantime, I have paperwork. There is a price to pay for working in an official capacity."

Gideon knew he had been dismissed. He rose from the chair, disappointed by Palmer's response. He wanted to do something immediately—that very moment, if he could. Action was the only way to ease the ache of his loss.

"I'll think about what you've said," Gideon replied. "While I'm considering my future career, I'm going to search by the river. If my sister was taken away by boat, someone might have seen it."

Palmer released a faint sigh, but didn't look up from his task. "Good luck."

"Luck is for people who don't put in the work."

The detective inspector laughed softly, as if he'd heard an echo from his own past. "Take it anyway."

CHAPTER 16

That night, Miranda timed her rendezvous at the airfield carefully. Close to midnight, the workers were long gone and only a handful of watchmen were present. It was also late enough she could slip out of the house undetected, using the aqueducts to reach the stables at the end of the street. From there, riding to her destination was easy.

She met Janey on the outskirts of the airfield. Crossing the property didn't worry Miranda much—the guards rarely patrolled the grounds since few people dreamed of stealing an airship. Most required a large and highly trained crew just to get it in the air. Instead, security was focused on the administration buildings, where the cash was kept. Miranda gave that section of the airfield a wide berth as they crept toward their destination.

"What are you wearing?" Janey asked, squinting in the dark.

"It's the latest in battle gear," Miranda replied, but offered no more than that. "There's the *Scorpion*."

"Oh." Janey made an appreciative noise. "Now then, isn't she a beauty?"

Miranda had named the ship after the tarot card she'd drawn

from Madam Alma's deck. It only made sense to borrow it, especially when it was perfect for what she had to do. As quietly as they could, the two women climbed aboard. The aether balloons were already full, simply waiting for the turn of a nozzle to top them up.

"This ship is just a little thing," Janey observed, looking around the deck.

"Two people can run it easily." Miranda pointed to the controls, explaining each feature as she went. "It's made for in-city flight. Placing one balloon above the other allows the ship to navigate narrow passages between buildings. There are lights to scan the ground. Catchers gently force the birds and dragons away from the propellers. And here are the levers to automatically release the mooring lines."

"Right you are," Janey said, running her hands over the controls as if exploring a new lover. "And we'll be searching the graveyard with the floodlights?"

"We've been searching in daylight, but every source I've consulted says that's not when the creatures are generally active," Miranda reasoned. "The *Scorpion* can fly low enough to see clearly while remaining high enough to remain safe."

"And hunt," Janey said.

"And hunt." Miranda took the aether weapon from its case, running her hand over the finely worked brass. Janey had etched a name in flowing script across the barrel—*Venom*. Miranda's fingers stilled. "You named it."

"I thought it fit," Janey said. "If you're the Scorpion, then this is your barb."

Miranda bit her lip. Her first thought was that naming a weapon seemed pompous—and impractical. Aether weapons, if used, would need to be regularly replaced. More to the point, it added to the Scorpion's story, and Miranda wasn't sure how much life she was ready to breathe into her persona.

Still, Venom was Janey's creation as much as her own. Naming it was her right. Miranda let her reservations go.

They took the ship up, Janey watching Miranda work the controls. The young woman was already a qualified pilot, so she didn't have much to learn. By the time they reached altitude, she could take over.

Unfortunately, the launch did not go unnoticed. Watchmen streamed across the field, waving their arms and shouting.

"Blast," Miranda muttered. She leaned over the side, bellowing for all she was worth. "Don't shoot! It's Miss Miranda. I'm stealing my father's ship for a few hours. Be good dears and don't tell him."

The men stopped in their tracks, pointing and waving their arms in a way that said they didn't get paid enough for such nonsense. It would have been amusing if Miranda weren't certain there would be hell to pay later.

She would worry about *later* once it arrived. Following Miranda's plan, they cruised low over the graveyard, using floodlights to search for movement. All they found were deer and rabbits, so they abandoned the lights, using the darkness as a disguise. After that, Janey steered the *Scorpion* through the streets bordering the graveyard. Eventually, they shifted east toward the river and scoured ramshackle alleyways Miranda had never seen before.

They drifted along in silence, the propellers still, using the night breeze and the buoyancy of the ship to move like a shadow. If Unseen were hunting those who could not defend themselves, this part of town was ideal territory. Miranda leaned over the side of the ship, rifle at the ready.

Something moved in the shadows. She tensed, sighting down Venom's barrel. But no, it was a dog rummaging in the trash. Raising her head, she squinted down with a frown. She was getting twitchy.

Eventually, the tangled streets of the slums opened to show the long expanse of the river's northern bank. There was nothing there but the occasional warehouse, dark and empty at this time of night. It was a lonely, almost desolate place.

Movement. Miranda nearly cried out.

Below, a band of Unseen flitted like shadows, moving from darkness to darkness in darting spurts of speed. She remembered Gideon's story about the men in charge when Sidonie was taken, but there was no sign of humans now. These creatures were on their own.

How had they entered the city? Gideon's questions about underground rivers and flaws in the barrier suddenly made sense. There had to be at least one spot where the Unseen could come and go. Perhaps not every monster knew it was there, but these did.

And why were they here? Was it simply to hunt?

Miranda saw a lone man walking ahead, moving west along the riverbank, oblivious to what trailed him. She pointed, and Janey quickly angled the *Scorpion* to intercept.

When the lights and propellers kicked to life, the man turned. Instantly, Miranda recognized Gideon. Horror crawled up her throat, cutting off her air. What the hell was he doing alone by the river so late at night? *Probably the same thing I am. Looking for clues.*

Miranda drew breath to shout a warning, but the creatures were too quick. They sprang from the shadows, blocking his escape. Gideon searched for an opening, but he didn't stand a chance. Like lions or hyenas, the Unseen tackled him to the ground. He fell with a bellow of surprise and fear.

Miranda fired, killing the hindmost in the pack. The others scattered in confusion. The reprieve lasted only a second, but it was enough for Gideon to rise and draw his weapon. It was an ordinary pistol, but he fired straight into the heart of his nearest assailant, dropping it in a shower of bone and gore. His second shot was not as lucky. It tore the creature's shoulder open, but pain seemed irrelevant to the creature. It sprang in a frenzy of claws and teeth.

Miranda fired twice more, holding the rest of the pack back as Gideon battled. Three of the creatures were dead and one wounded, but half a dozen remained. She and Gideon were outnumbered three to one, but the tide had turned. The Unseen milled, afraid of the deadly weapons and the bright lights from the sky—all except one.

That one crouched, glaring up at Miranda with eyes that reflected the ship's lights like a cat. When it barked an order, the others stilled, cowering like puppies. Clearly, this one was the leader, and it was re-evaluating its tactics. Terror fluttered in Miranda's stomach.

A gunshot sounded, and Gideon's assailant fell. Her brother was bent nearly double, clearly winded from the fight but slowly retreating. One step, two steps. Slow and steady. Getting some distance from the pack. Once he turned and ran, the Unseen's instinct to chase would take over. He'd be nothing more than prey after that.

She counted her breaths, wondering how long she could hold the leader's gaze. Three steps, four steps. Then Gideon glanced up at the airship that had come to his aid. Recognition lit his face.

"Miranda, what the bloody hell?" he exploded, shattering the charmed silence.

The Unseen surged, their discipline broken. Miranda panicked for a split second, her vision swirling like a kaleidoscope before she gathered her concentration.

Gideon fired again, but he had to be low on ammunition. She caught her breath, bracing against the side of the ship, and began shooting. By the time the third Unseen had dropped, the others had fled to the shadows, out of her line of sight. So had her brother. She swore, frantic to confirm he was all right.

"Something's wrong," Janey shouted. "There's a drag on the ship I can't explain."

Miranda focused on the ship. She felt the force, too, as if a hand was pressing the *Scorpion* to the earth. Janey worked the controls, trying every trick to break free.

"What's wrong?" Miranda asked, shouting above the grinding engine.

"I don't know," Janey called back. "It's like we're in a net."

How was this possible? Could the Unseen wield magic? The Conclave had always denied it, but was that a lie?

The ship tilted wildly as Miranda tried to fix her aim on the leader of the Unseen. As she did, the creature got to its feet, glaring upward with bared teeth. With surprise, Miranda saw it was female, beautiful in a bizarre way, with hair streaked a reddish-brown. The gown she wore hung on her skeletal figure, but it was only a few years out of fashion.

The dress unnerved Miranda. It was too human, too feminine. That gave them common ground, and Miranda would have none of it.

The ship lurched again, almost skimming the ground. Miranda stumbled to her knees, fear making her gasp. The Unseen female below continued to stare, reinforcing the idea she was somehow behind the ship's malfunction. Bracing herself, Miranda fired, hoping to at least break the leader's concentration. The shot landed inches from the creature's feet, making it—*her*—skip away.

The ship lurched again, but the downward pressure resumed a moment later. Miranda had to do something before they crashed. She jumped over the side, landing on the grass.

"Get back on the ship," Janey shouted.

Miranda was acutely aware there were other Unseen in the area, but there was no way to aim with the ship bobbing like a bar of soap in a toddler's bath. The female Unseen wavered before her, as if unsure whether to attack or run. She was smeared with blood, her wild hair falling free to her waist. The creature gave an angry, desperate howl.

Miranda raised Venom. The creature rushed her with a bloodcurdling snarl. Miranda fired, aiming for the center of her chest. At that range, it was impossible to miss. A hole appeared in the female's bodice like a pinprick of black. Immediately, smoke began pouring from the wound as if she were burning from within. She undulated a moment, as if buffeted by an invisible wave, and then seemed to collapse inward. A second later, the creature was on the ground, ribs exposed to the night and her chest a crumbling shell. She had died soundlessly, lungs gone before she could even scream. Smoke and steam curled upward, faint wisps against the darkness.

Miranda stared numbly at the ruin, her eyes roving over each pale limb. The Unseen's slack face appeared almost human in death. Miranda knelt to examine the body more closely, noting the sharp teeth showing between parted lips and the curved talons of its claws.

Miranda began to shake, as if she'd suddenly contracted a fever. She barely heard Janey's cry of relief when the *Scorpion* righted itself in the air. Angrily, Miranda wiped hot tears from her cheeks.

She forced herself to regard the corpse. This was the enemy. She'd dealt with it for tonight. No doubt she would have to do it again. Still afraid to touch the dead thing, as if it could possibly leap up again, she nudged the left hand with Venom's point, noticing a glint of metal.

The creature wore a ring.

Another wave of nausea left Miranda lightheaded. It looked like a betrothal ring wreathed in tiny filigree flowers—surely it had come from a victim? Was it a clue to one of the many disappearances? Was there a family waiting for news of their missing daughter? Swiftly, she drew it from the creature's hand and shoved it in her pocket. Then she spun away, wondering where her brother had gone.

The shadows seemed alive, as if a prickling energy ran through them. Or perhaps it was through her. The ague of shock had drained away, leaving her senses sharp. She spun toward movement to her right.

It was Gideon, his eyes wild from battle. Miranda took one running step toward him before freezing in place. Something about the way he held himself put a barrier between them. It took her a moment to understand he was furious.

"I killed one more. The other one ran," he said in response to her unasked question. "We're safe enough for the moment."

His gaze flicked to the creature's smoking body, then to Miranda. "Explain."

"Searching by air is faster. We've always searched by day, but that's not when the creatures come out."

His mouth thinned. For an unsettling instant, he resembled their father in one of his moods. "Clearly, you had a plan for the monsters once you found them."

Miranda suppressed the impulse to hide Venom behind her back. "I came prepared."

"You could have been killed," he said quietly. "I couldn't bear to lose you as well."

"No more than I want to lose my brother. Why are you here?"

"There's a chance Sidonie's kidnappers might have taken her away by boat."

Miranda hadn't thought of that. "Did you find any clues?"

"No. It seems the clues found me."

"Are you hurt?"

"No."

"You're lucky."

"I've been trained." He rubbed his face, clearly exhausted. "I've been over the wall. I've had practice."

Miranda tensed. "And you're about to point out that I haven't."

He heaved a sigh. "You're destined for something else. Something better than fighting in the streets."

His words swept away everything she'd set in motion, as if she'd been playing a game. Resentment tightened her jaw. "You couldn't just thank me for saving your skin?" She regretted the outburst as soon as it left her tongue, but it was too late.

"Thank you."

It wasn't sarcasm. Not quite. His voice held layers of emotion Miranda barely understood. Guilt. Fear. Remorse. Anger. Somewhere in the mix was resentment.

Slow realization left her cold. "You blame yourself for what happened to Sidonie."

"Of course, I do." His eyes blazed with frustration. "I knew what was happening in the city. I should have done something before now. I should have been able to save her."

"You can't think that." Miranda shook her head. "It will drive you mad."

He cast her a hard look. "You're a fine one to talk. You stole a ship. Who is your crew?"

With that, he took her arm and marched her toward the hovering vessel. Wary of his mood, Miranda let herself be led. It was only a matter of time before someone—or something—stumbled across the scene, and she had no intention of being caught next to a smoking corpse. "Stealing is relative. I am a Fletcher, after all, and it's our ship to use."

He spun her so they faced each other. She caught her breath, more from surprise than physical pain, although his grip was firm.

"This is not a joke," he said through clenched teeth. "I won't have your death on my conscience, too."

Gideon glared down at her, and she felt his need to protect

her beneath the surface of his fury. He loved her as only a big brother could.

It was the only reason she forgave him.

Miranda pulled her arm free, then took a step back. For the first time she could remember, there was a wedge between her and Gideon, but she didn't have the strength to fix it. Not tonight.

"Let's go home," she said.

$\mathcal{M}$iranda did not sleep. Instead, the battle played over and over in her mind, pouncing just as exhaustion sought to claim her. Sometimes, the Unseen woman caught Miranda and sank her claws deep, tearing flesh from bone. Other times, the carnage went wild, with a thousand bodies lying bloody on the ground, and more fangs and claws tearing innocents asunder. In the worst of her imaginings, she saw Gideon fall, unable to get back up.

The Unseen had always been caricatures to her, but this female was different. She was an individual—a distinct threat rather than a vague horde of bogeymen locked outside the wall. She had a dress and a ring and a terrifying power that had nearly wrecked the ship.

Miranda had ripped away her life.

She curled up in her bed, hugging her knees close as tears leaked from under her lashes. She'd saved her brother's life, but she wondered what she'd done to her own.

The night's work had ended as well as could be expected. Janey had landed the *Scorpion* safely at the airfield. When Gideon had emerged from the ship, the watchmen had been greatly reassured. They'd all made it home in one piece, though Gideon had gained some bad cuts and bruises in the fight.

It came as no surprise when Miranda was called to her father's office the next morning. Fletcher sat behind his desk wearing a belligerent scowl. He'd shaken the head cold, but he was still not back to full strength.

"I heard you were out with Gideon on the *Scorpion* last night," he announced. "Your brother had no business allowing you to go, and you should have known better."

Miranda nodded mutely, too surprised to reply. Gideon had taken the blame for the *Scorpion's* adventure. He was protecting her again, even though she was an adult woman. He trod a fine line between endearing and frustrating in the extreme.

"It was an unauthorized flight," her father said. "You might have been hurt. You might have crashed the ship. What if the watchmen had fired on you?"

"None of those things happened," Miranda said reasonably.

Heaving a sigh, he sat forward to sip the cup peppermint tea that sat steaming on his desk, no doubt prescribed for his digestion. His stomach had been touchy since the engagement ball. After making a face, he pushed the cup away. "If you and Gideon took the *Scorpion* like thieves in the night, then you both knew you were in the wrong."

She opened her mouth to say the entire escapade had been her idea, but Gideon entered the office. He had a bruise on his face, but nothing worse was visible.

"What's all this?" Gideon asked.

Fletcher's color was high. "Miranda about to explain why you two stole a ship last night."

"We were searching for Unseen," Gideon replied smoothly. "We found a pack of them near the river."

"Where else did you fly?" Fletcher asked Gideon, not even looking at Miranda.

Stubbornly, she spoke up. "I used a wide search pattern, then moved east once we'd covered the cemetery. There was nothing of interest until we reached the riverbank."

Miranda kept her face neutral as Gideon shot her a quelling look. He'd warned her last night against revealing the full extent of her involvement. Even if she'd saved Gideon, Fletcher would never forgive her for willfully taking such a risk. Gideon was probably right, but the secret chafed.

"Are you certain it was Unseen you saw by the river?" Fletcher asked.

Gideon paled at the memory. "Yes. A pack of them. I'm sure the female was the creature who killed Black."

That startled Miranda. "Are you certain?"

Gideon made a helpless gesture. "When they first chased me, she spoke. I'm sure of it."

"She *spoke*?" Fletcher rose, circling the desk.

"I don't know." Gideon ran a hand through his hair. "She wanted revenge because I shot her mate."

"Was that why they came into the city?" Miranda asked. "To find you?"

"Fantasy," Fletcher said flatly.

Miranda thought of the ring. Jewelry had meaning. The female had definitely been enough of a person to feel hate. "There is a lot about the Unseen we don't understand."

Fletcher finally regarded her. "Is understanding required?"

It was a plea. Ignorance was safer. The Conclave would be especially displeased to hear about Unseen wielding magic. The significance of that detail felt like an explosive about to ignite.

She took her father's hand and squeezed it. "People are in danger. Our own family has been attacked. We had to do something."

Fletcher's face furrowed with concern. "Will anything tie you to the bodies?"

"No." Gideon folded his arms. "And if I were a betting man, I'd wager they were gone before dawn broke. From what I've seen in the Outlands, the monsters reclaim their dead for food."

Fletcher nodded, his expression grim. "Promise me you'll say nothing about any of this. Ormond already has his eyes on us."

"But people need to be warned," Miranda objected. "It's not safe to walk the streets at night."

Her father frowned. "Let me deal with it."

"Or I can," Gideon said. "I'm in contact with Inspector Palmer. I'm going to begin work as an inquiry agent."

Fletcher whirled on him. "You'll do no such thing. Have you heard *nothing* I've said?"

Gideon swallowed. "Whatever Ormond wants, I can't carry on as if nothing happened. Sidonie's still missing."

Miranda heard the guilt in his words, the unspoken *if only*. By the pain in his eyes, Fletcher heard it, too.

"My boy," Fletcher began, but he stopped. Miranda saw the objections cross his face—the family's survival, the business, the safety of the children he still had. "I can't let you do that. While you're under my roof, you'll do as I say."

"Then that's the first change I need to make," Gideon stated, his voice hard.

He slammed the door as he left.

No one saw Gideon again that day, or the next. Fletcher was unusually closemouthed to Olivia and Miranda. Even so, it was plain the rift between father and son went deeper than what Miranda had witnessed. Finally, on All Hallows' Eve, she received a note from Gideon informing her that he'd rented the rooms above Dobson's bookshop and would be sleeping there for the foreseeable future.

When Miranda went to his bedroom, some of his clothes were missing. She packed a suitcase with more shoes, shirts, and the necessaries men never thought about, and then had Jackson drop her at the bookshop. Dobson looked up from his desk when she came through the door. They locked eyes for a second, then the bookseller pulled off his wire-rimmed spectacles.

"Good day, Miss Miranda." His lined face was sympathetic. Obviously, he knew at least part of their story. "I believe Mr. Fletcher is at home."

She left the suitcase at the bottom of the stairs, deciding Gideon could lug it up at his leisure, and ascended the steps. Gideon was waiting for her by the time she reached the top.

"You great idiot," she said, folding him in an embrace. The solid warmth and familiarity of his form was like a balm. Although he'd only just left, she already missed him with her whole heart. There had been four siblings in the house so recently, and now there were only two.

"I know it's hard," he said, "but it's for the best. If I'm not on speaking terms with my family, no one can blame Father for what I do."

"What are you talking about?"

"The Conclave. Father said Ormond is watching, and our friends from the Citadel don't want anyone investigating a breach in the barrier."

Miranda's breath caught, grasping the logic behind his desertion. "Does Father know your reasoning?"

"Of course not. He's too forthright to keep up a lie."

Tears caught in Miranda's throat. "You shouldn't need to do this."

"We'll see. Come inside."

The rooms were small and simple but more pleasant than she'd expected. There was a bedroom and a front room, which served as a combination dining room, parlor, and office.

"What's this?" she asked, studying a wall covered with newspaper clippings and other scraps of paper.

"Everything I could find about disappearances in the last few years," he said. "The majority were our age."

There were a few photographs, but mostly small articles from the newspaper—a few lines, but not much more. The press had been spare with details, and now she could guess why—they didn't dare displease men like Ormond. Altogether, she counted eighteen missing persons. Some were just names and dates written on a piece of paper. Others were smiling faces captured in sepia. John Bartman's name was there. As was Sidonie's, of course.

"Those are just the ones I know about," Gideon said. He grimaced ruefully. "Inspector Palmer suspects there are many more."

Scanning the names and faces left a hollow place inside her, as if their absence found an answering abyss where her innocence had once been. Miranda pulled her attention away. "How will you afford to live?" she asked.

"I'm not taking a penny from Father. The less contact we have, the better for us both."

"He wouldn't feel that way," Miranda said quickly.

Gideon shook his head. "Palmer is referring clients to me. My first case, ironically, is a runaway son. In this instance, I think he actually ran away."

"Do you think you can find him?"

"Yes, probably in an East End tavern. I'll have him back before he catches fleas." Gideon wandered to the Welsh dresser serving as his pantry. It struck her that, despite everything, he seemed relaxed, happy even. He'd found a purpose beyond fulfilling Fletcher's plans for his heir.

"Would you like some tea?" Gideon asked.

"Yes, please," she said, thinking of the last time they'd come to Dobson's to see a map. It seemed an exceptionally long time ago. "You know, we still don't know how the Unseen are getting through the barrier."

Gideon handed her a cup. It was faded, but free of chips. "Or why the Conclave doesn't simply fix it. My missing persons are just one of many mysteries."

"I know it seems as if the missing are connected to the breach in the barrier, but we don't know that for certain."

"The Unseen are working with someone," Gideon said. "We just don't know who—or why they left me alive, unless it was so that they could kill me that night on the riverbank."

And we still don't know whether Sidonie is really dead. Neither said it, but the question was there all the same. Miranda could see the guilt in his eyes again, and she hated it.

"I have something you might be interested in," she said, opening her reticule and drawing out the ring she'd taken from the dead creature. "I took it from the female Unseen. She must have stolen it—maybe from a victim. I wondered if you could find the owner. It's quite unique."

When she put it in his palm, he turned it over, studying the dainty filigree. "I feel as if I've seen this before," he said. "I'll look into it."

Then he set it aside, growing serious. "Miranda, I've done you a great disservice by involving you in this matter. I shouldn't have done it."

"Nonsense," she said flatly. "You've always encouraged me to stretch myself. It turns out that's a rare compliment."

"And yet perhaps I had no right to urge you on. Taking the *Scorpion* was a huge risk, not to mention, um, everything else you did that night."

"You're not responsible for my actions, or their consequences," she said, her voice growing quiet. "You don't get to blame yourself for anything I do."

But as his dark blue eyes held hers, she saw the fear in them. He'd been happy to support her when there was only a minor risk of trouble, but now he'd lost his twin and the Conclave was watching the people he loved. Allowing Miranda to roam free wasn't half so attractive now.

What Gideon didn't see was she needed to act, just as he did. Both Gideon and Fletcher risked losing their family by holding on too tight. They were more similar than they knew.

"I saw a photograph that was sent to the police and newspaper," he said unexpectedly. "Or what was left of the photograph. The Conclave ordered them all burned. Now the police are hunting for the sender and it won't end well once the Conclave has their hands on that person."

"Are there any clues?"

"It was an Unseen killed with an aether weapon. The burns are distinctive."

Despite herself, Miranda shivered. It was plain from his expression that Gideon guessed it had been her. If he hadn't known before he'd seen Viper in action, he did now. She tried to swallow the lump in her throat, but the fear lodged fast, pulsing with every beat of her heart.

"Have a care, Miranda," he said. "You'll push past the point where I can protect you."

It felt like a threat as much as a warning. She refused to heed it. "I can't turn back time."

A tiny part of her wished she could. When they'd first come to this shop, she and Gideon had been united. They had grown since then, but change was pulling them apart.

He leaned forward, his expression earnest. "I beg you, don't put yourself—and the family—at risk."

She set down her tea, sorrow sharp inside her. "Then let me help you with your investigations."

A silence followed as he searched her face. Finally, he shook his head. "That's how we got here in the first place. I can't trust you to stay in the background."

Disconcerted, Miranda glanced down at her hands, where they were folded in her lap. They curled into fists as cold anger burned through to her core. "In the background," she repeated, barely believing what she'd heard.

"For Father's sake. For Olivia's. Father's old, and she can't see past her studies. Someone has to look after them."

But why did that someone have to be Miranda?

"Don't blame me for speaking the truth." He caught her wrist. "Don't let this come between us."

She smiled, but it was an empty gesture. "Don't apologize unless you mean it."

He dropped his hand from her arm as they both rose, suddenly watchful of one another. The wedge between them had become as profound as the Conclave's barrier.

"Please, Gideon, don't shut me out," she pleaded, breaking the horrible silence. "Please. Neither of us can face this fight alone."

Gideon's face twisted a moment, but then he heaved a sigh. "Bloody hell, Miranda."

Another leaden quiet fell between them. Miranda silently cursed as she felt the prick of tears. "Think about it," she insisted, briskly kissing him on the cheek. "You know where I am."

An ache throbbed in her chest as she turned and left, retreating down the stairs and past the suitcase she had brought. Mr. Dobson was with a customer, so she exited without a word. That was just as well, for her heart was breaking. Up until this minute, Gideon had always been her best ally.

It was true she had others—Janey and Mrs. Randall, and perhaps even Kitteridge. They'd each helped her, but those friendships were still new. They weren't her brother.

Miranda stopped at the corner, taking a deep breath and fighting back her grief. Ever since Sidonie had vanished, Miranda had known the future would be difficult. She hadn't expected it to hurt in so many different ways.

But however much that grief mattered, the heartbreak would be far worse if she turned back now. Now that she knew what she could do, she had no excuse to walk away. Not when she could take action that mattered. Gideon wasn't the only one who'd lost a sister.

Miranda marched down the winding street toward Hellion House, her boot heels sounding firm against the cobblestones. She had a war to fight. Dangerous enemies. Monsters to hunt.

The day of the Scorpion had come, and this was its dawn.

THE END

The adventure continues in *Leopard Ascending*.

Did you miss Miranda and Gideon's first adventure in *Fortune's Eve*? Turn the page for an excerpt!

FORTUNE'S EVE

A HELLION HOUSE SHORT STORY

by Emma Jane Holloway

Copyright © 2019

he Outlands
Late September

"If we don't find the wreck soon, we'll be obliged to turn back," Norton Fletcher said.

Gideon glanced at the sky, calculating the remaining daylight. His father was right. No one risked traveling outside the city after dark. "That would be certain death for the crew of the wreck."

"But not for us." Fletcher's face was rigid. "Don't get caught up in the emotion of these missions. It's a quick way to die."

Gideon gave a low laugh to hide his resentment. His father never let go of his impulse to instruct his grown son. "I have compassion."

"A waste of energy. Everything breaks and everything mends," Fletcher said. "Live long enough, and you'll understand."

"Do you truly believe that?" Gideon asked, heat creeping into his words.

"Yes," his father replied, "and no. It's what old men tell themselves to stop the ache of fear in their bellies."

The words were terse, a bitter blend of the flippant and the true. Questions crowded Gideon's mind, but Fletcher's expression closed like a door banging shut, the *Dragonfly*'s captain replacing his father. Not that the difference was pronounced on most days.

Gideon studied his father, who stood at the pilot's station with feet planted wide and back ramrod straight. Fletcher wasn't a large man, but his stocky figure and lined features, weathered by decades of sun and wind, made Gideon think of petrified oak. As Fletcher eased a lever forward, the *Dragonfly* dipped closer to the river, twin propellers *thwop-thwopping* through the mist. Autumn fog trailed ghostly fingers around the dirigible as if the mist meant to snatch it from the sky.

A flare had gone up two hours ago, according to the report of the watchmen who scanned the forest from the great towers that flanked the city gates. Fletcher Industries—one of the premier airship firms in the city—kept half-a-dozen rescue crafts on standby, but the last week had been busy. When word arrived, only the *Dragonfly* was docked at the airfield and the crews were shorthanded. Norton Fletcher—owner, designer, and still one of the best pilots in the sky—had taken the job himself. Of course, Gideon went with him. He was heir to the Fletcher empire and familiar with the day-to-day operations, but he still took pleasure in watching his father work. Or he had. As the afternoon wore on, that first thrill had darkened to anxiety. So far, they hadn't found any trace of the wreck.

Gideon peered over the edge of the gondola, estimating the distance to the dense treetops. Ash, birch, oak, chestnut, and the occasional conifer grew in a lush tangle. This area between settlements was called the Outlands. After the population fled the countryside, nature had thrown a party. The result was the beautiful but deadly forest that covered every trace of civilization.

Gideon leaned out another inch, one hand on a sturdy cable. There was still plenty of clearance before the craft risked scraping the branches, but distance made it hard to see the river. Unfortunately, closing the gap would be unwise. That was the gamble with rescue missions—risk all to save the innocent, yet risk becoming a victim oneself.

A trio of dragons soared above the branches as the ship passed overhead. Their population had grown with the forest, but the city dwellers paid them no heed. Urban dragons were relatively small, weighing about twenty pounds. Even their wild cousins rarely grew larger than a goat, and humanity had far more to worry about than an invasive species of lizard.

For the hundredth time that afternoon, the broad silver swath of the river emerged from the encroaching trees. The *Dragonfly* had followed a zigzagging path, searching both sides of the water. They had seen a fleet of River Rats—clans of wandering thieves and magicians who lived aboard their crafts—and once a smuggler's ship with its gun ports open. Both had probably been bound for the walled farms to the east. There was gold in river business—at least for those brave enough to risk it. Gideon would take the sky any day.

The foliage slipped from view, the water gleaming directly below. His heart skipped as he saw what the *Dragonfly* had come for—the wreckage of a midsized sailing craft.

"There," Gideon cried, pointing over the side. "Bring the ship around again."

The crew—four hands besides the Fletchers—jumped to obey, hauling on the lines that adjusted the auxiliary sails. Boilers hissed, feeding the engine that drove the propellers. Slowly, the *Dragonfly*, with its twin gray-and-white silk balloons, pivoted in the sky.

"Sir, we dare not go lower," Higgins, the grizzled senior airman, said.

"Then get your gear on," Norton Fletcher replied, guiding the ship into position above the wreck. "We'll go down for a look, although it's not promising."

Hopeful or not, it was still their duty to search for survivors. Gideon grabbed his own equipment, wondering what they'd find. Fools had a way of getting what they deserved.

The river—cold, fast, and often foggy—was riddled with ruined weirs and the stumps of old bridges. Wise travelers took a River Rat who knew the water's tricks. According to the harbormaster's records—all crafts were required to declare their routes and crews before they cast off—Mr. Joseph Ellery, esquire, had not. On some level, Gideon wasn't surprised. He'd met the weedy banker at parties and the theater, and he had been consistently underwhelmed.

By the time the *Dragonfly* hovered in place, Gideon, Higgins, and Crewman Yale were ready to descend. Flight crews typically wore supple leather suits as protection from wind and weather, along with high boots and close-fitting helmets. Gideon added a weapons belt and a rifle in a sling across his back, as well as long knives strapped to his thighs.

"You've got an hour of good daylight left," Fletcher said. "Don't waste it."

Gideon tried to catch his father's eye, but the goggles that protected against the burn of the wind made it impossible. He wasn't sure why he bothered to grasp at that last moment of connection—he needed no reassurance, and emotional displays were not his family's way. Still, the unknown that lurked below left a hollow feeling in his gut. When Higgins offered him a flask of smuggled French brandy, Gideon gratefully took a swig for luck.

A square metal plate, about five feet across, formed part of the *Dragonfly*'s main deck. Once unlocked from thick steel hasps, the platform could be raised and lowered with steam-powered efficiency. Cables spooled onto four large wheels that moved on a single automated crank calibrated to keep the plate perfectly level—a key feature of Norton Fletcher's design. The rescue crew mounted the platform, crouching low and grasping the lines for balance while Fletcher himself released the brake. With a whir of well-oiled gears, they gently floated the forty feet to the river's edge.

A breeze caught the platform, swaying it slightly, but Gideon didn't mind. The scent of greenery and rich mud was a novelty, one he inhaled with gratitude. His home stank of smoke and too many bodies crowded close together for protection. The Outlands might be deadly, but at least they were clean.

The men jumped the last few feet, boots splashing in the shallow water. The wreck was in the middle of the river, but there wasn't enough of the ship left for survivors to take shelter in it. The crew would have struck out for dry ground or been carried off by the current. As this was the closer bank, it made sense to begin the search here.

"By our calculations, that's where the flare was fired," Higgins said, pointing a dozen yards ahead. "Anyone hoping for rescue wouldn't go far."

Gideon nodded agreement and scrambled up the bank, not wasting time. He pushed up his goggles, needing his peripheral vision now. As the September shadows lengthened, the fog already misted above the water. It would be dusk long before the sun actually set.

Unholstering his rifle, Gideon strode onward, using his nose as well as his eyes and ears. Death had a smell, as did blood, but the wind was off the river and gave him no clues. A rustle in the trees caught his attention.

"Ellery? Hello?"

Gideon raised the rifle and turned slowly, realizing there had been birdsong a moment ago, but now there was none. Somewhere in the treetops, a dragon squawked and flapped in seeming fury. Gideon began to sweat, soaking the shirt beneath his jacket. He was still on the bank, the bush and trees barely a dozen yards away and hiding who knew what. Countless ruins lay buried along the riverside, evidence of a world before walls and the terror of the Unseen.

Gideon swept his rifle in a slow arc, his nerves alive with dread. "Ellery?"

The woods to his left exploded with movement and sound. He swiveled toward it, but was a beat too late. He had a swift impression of rags and bony limbs, but his senses failed. A long shriek of rage split the silence as the thing hurtled through the air, arms extended. Gideon had no chance to aim.

Crewman Yale's rifle cracked, smoke belching from the muzzle. The attacking figure flew sideways, the force of the shot tearing a hole through its chest. The scream faded to a gurgle as its lungs failed, but the bubbling moan didn't stop. The thing writhed, trying to turn over so it could crawl. The Unseen weren't immortal, but they were extremely hard to kill.

Gideon registered the pale face and wide eyes, the sharp and blackened teeth. The Unseen hated daylight, but they'd brave it for an easy kill—which he'd been a moment ago. Barely aware of its mortal wounds, the creature made it to its hands and knees, gazing at him with hungry rapture.

Gideon blew its head off. He watched it drop, still twitching, as bile rose in his throat. He swallowed it down, icy and sweating at the same time.

Yale came to stand beside him. "You're lucky, sir. It was one of the crazy ones."

"Lucky?" Gideon echoed.

The crewman pulled a face. "It's the smart ones you have to fear. Those will do worse than gnaw your bones."

Gideon stared at the bloody ground—at the bits of gore scattering the weeds. The Unseen weren't the only horrors in the woods, but they were the most common. No one knew where the creatures originated from, why they had appeared after the Great Disaster, or even exactly what they were. Men of science agreed they were living beings, and yet unlike any other species. They were perfect predators that had driven humanity from the countryside, defeating every army kings and generals threw at them. A sudden urge to run swept over Gideon, but he stood his ground, clenching his teeth to stop the chatter.

"Sir?" Yale asked, casting him a concerned glance.

Brutally, Gideon shoved the nightmare down to the cellars of his soul. "I'm fine."

Higgins gave a sharp whistle. He'd stayed close to the platform, guarding their escape. Yale and Gideon turned to see another figure, this one using a rifle as a cane, limping from the trees. It was Ellery, hurt and clearly exhausted.

Gideon broke into a run, lengthening his stride to close the distance. "Where's your crew?"

"Gone," Ellery panted. "We were separated in the wreck. The captain fired a flare to summon aid, but no other ships came. The men never stood a chance. I just saw what was left."

"You went into the forest?" Gideon asked, incredulous. "How did you survive?"

"I had to know it was over for them. I couldn't just walk away."

"And what did you plan to do if you found them?"

The man was clearly an idiot. Entering the forest meant walking into the jaws of death.

"It's irrelevant now." Ellery peered over his shoulder with the air of a man who'd seen his own grave. The Unseen dragged their meals beneath the trees, where they stripped the flesh like hungry jackals. Ellery's nauseated expression filled in the details.

Gideon wrapped an arm around the man, half-carrying him toward the ship's platform. If Ellery was the sole survivor, all that remained was to return to the *Dragonfly* and safety. Higgins stood on guard a dozen feet away. Already on the platform, Yale raised his rifle to cover their retreat.

Three Unseen burst from the woods, thin limbs barely covered by fluttering rags. One howled like the first creature, but the other two were silent, their eyes calculating. As Yale had said, the smart ones were dangerous. Gideon heaved Ellery across his shoulders and ran.

Yale fired, but only winged his target. Two of the Unseen dropped to all fours, springing forward like wolves. Gideon pushed faster, stumbling beneath Ellery's weight and cursing as the rifle slipped from his grasp. He let it drop, not daring to slow down and retrieve it. Seconds counted now.

Higgins was closest and shot once, twice, but went down under the weight of the Unseen. Gideon heaved Ellery to the platform before turning back to help. Yale was already beside Higgins, dragging one attacker away. Gideon drew his sidearm, intending to shoot the second.

The thing's head jerked up as if it had read his thoughts. Hate-filled eyes scorched him as the creature sprang toward the rifle Gideon had dropped. A smart one, then. It snatched up the weapon, raising it awkwardly. The sight filled Gideon with a new kind of horror. His pistol roared just as the beast pulled the trigger. The rifle shot skyward as the Unseen dropped, the back of its skull shattered, but the fight wasn't over. A second creature lunged, hot and horrible breath fanning Gideon's face. He bashed the butt of his weapon into its jaw, knocking the creature sideways. The pistol slipped from Gideon's hand, spinning away. The Unseen staggered, but regained its balance in a single, dance-like shuffle. Gideon slid one of his knives from its sheath. As the creature surged again, he drove the blade deep between its ribs, twisting until he found the heart. This time, it went down.

Yale had killed the third Unseen, then heaved Higgins to the platform. Gideon grabbed his weapons before jumping aboard. Yale threw the lever that signaled the *Dragonfly*. With a click and a spin of gears, the platform began rising skyward. Gideon sat down hard, panting with exhaustion and relief. Below, Unseen littered the riverbank like broken mannequins. *One of them tried to use the rifle*, Gideon mused, but then pushed the idea away. Intelligence made them too human for comfort.

Higgins was on his knees, staring at his arm. The leather of his sleeve was torn from wrist to elbow, exposing a strip of skin. There, a perfect bite mark stood out in an angry red, a bruise already purpling around it.

"I'll clean the wound when we get to the ship," Gideon offered.

"No time," the man said, pulling off his helmet. The shorn gray hair stood out from his skull in sweat-drenched tufts. He drew a knife from his belt, then poised it above the wound.

Gideon grabbed the crewman's wrist, stopping him. The aftermath of the fight had left a tremor in his fingers, but pride was irrelevant now. Only Higgins mattered, a crewman who had flown into hell to rescue an innocent.

"That's just a myth," Gideon said. "The Unseen are living creatures. Another species. Medicine has proved you can't catch a disease that turns you into one of them."

The look the man gave Gideon was worse than any blow. What the gentry called superstitions were guideposts the workers used to make sense of their world. Gideon released his grip, suddenly conscious of overstepping a boundary. He was the captain's son, but Higgins was his own master.

"There's rules," Yale said. "It's the airman's way."

The knife bit deep, slicing beneath the broken skin in Higgins's arm. The breath hissed between the crewman's teeth, but he held the blade steady as he carved and lifted the mark away.

Yale drew his kerchief, folding it into a bandage as he waited. "It doesn't matter what the so-called doctors put in their reports. A man has to know he's clean."

Gideon looked away from the spectacle, barely seeing the misty treetops as they ascended. Emotions twisted inside him, fumbling for a truth he couldn't yet define. The sight of the blood, of the crewman carving his own flesh, filled him with angry confusion. Then his gaze fell on Ellery, who was massaging his swelling ankle. His crew had been eaten, his rescuers attacked, yet he'd escaped with no more than a sprain? Why was he whole when the members of his crew—and his rescuers —were not?

"Why the bloody hell were you out there?" Gideon snapped, giving way to rage. "Why risk a river passage? That's not for amateurs."

Ellery ducked his chin. "I've done it before. Running into that piling was pure bad luck."

Bad luck. Higgins, sweating and pale, was done with the knife. Yale bound his arm. Gideon tried to keep what was left of his calm by watching Ellery's expression. The man had the look of someone frozen in horror, as if his time in the woods kept repeating over and over behind his eyes.

"And the crew?"

"I used up my ammunition to save them." Ellery swallowed hard. "I was stranded. There was nothing more I could do except choose how to die."

Gideon digested Ellery's words. There was no doubt the man was devastated, but something didn't add up. "I wasn't aware you'd made the river passage before. The harbormaster said nothing about it."

But perhaps that was the point. Ellery had money, and the only reason a rich man would risk his life on the water was to hide something.

"Why the secrecy?" Gideon asked. "You know there will be an inquest after this."

"I do." Ellery's attention shifted away to the fog-shrouded trees. Sweat trickled from under the edge of his helmet, highlighting the pale blue veins beneath the skin. "Not all the monsters are in the forest."

"What does that mean?"

The man's green gaze slid over to pierce Gideon. "Make up your mind once the time comes."

CONTINUE the story in *Fortune's Eve*.

AFTERWORD

What *has* become of Sidonie? The answer lies in *Leopard Ascending*, the first novel in the Hellion House series. Many, many thanks to everyone who has joined the journey so far. I promise more airships, detectives, dragons, and Mr. Kitteridge's secret are all to come.

Read More from Emma Jane Holloway

www.EmmaJaneHolloway.com

Join the newsletter for exclusive updates and watch for upcoming releases in the Hellion House series, including *Leopard Ascending, Hellion's Journey* and more.

ALSO BY EMMA JANE HOLLOWAY

Hellion House Series

Fortune's Eve

Scorpion Dawn

Leopard Ascending

Hellion's Journey

Queen's Tide

Hellion Afternoon

Baskerville Affair series

A Study in Silks

A Study in Darkness

A Study in Ashes

The Baskerville Tales

The Baskerville Affair Complete Series

Audiobook

A Study in Silks

A Study in Darkness

A Study in Ashes

ABOUT THE AUTHOR

Ever since childhood, USA Today Bestselling Author Emma Jane Holloway refused to accept that history was nothing but facts prisoned behind the closed door of time. Why waste a perfectly good playground coloring within the timelines? Accordingly, her novels are filled with whimsical impossibilities and the occasional eye-blinking impertinence—but always in the service of grand adventure.

Struggling between the practical and the artistic—a family tradition, along with ghosts and a belief in the curative powers of shortbread—Emma Jane has a degree in literature and job in finance. She lives in the Pacific Northwest in a house crammed with black cats, books, musical instruments, and half-finished sewing projects. In the meantime, she's published articles, essays, short stories, and novels, including *The Baskerville Affair* novels, featuring the niece of Sherlock Holmes.

PRAISE FOR EMMA JANE HOLLOWAY

Magic, machines, mystery, mayhem, and all the danger one expects when people's loves and fears collide.

— KEVIN HEARNE

Holloway takes us for quite a ride, as her plot snakes through an alternative Victorian England full of intrigue, romance, murder, and tiny sandwiches.

— NICOLE PEELER, THE JANE TRUE SERIES

As Sherlock Holmes' niece, investigating murder while navigating the complicated shoals of Society—and romance—in an alternate Victorian England, Evelina Cooper is a charming addition to the canon.

— JACQUELINE CAREY

Splendid… the characters are thoroughly charming and the worldbuilding is first-rate

— ROMANTIC TIMES BOOK REVIEWS

Holloway stuffs her adventure with an abundance of characters and ideas and fills her heroine with talents and graces, all within a fun, brisk narrative.

— PUBLISHERS WEEKLY

Scorpion Dawn © 2019 Naomi Lester

Cover by Sly Fox Cover Designs

Editing by Cynthia Shepp

✿ Created with Vellum